CHILDREN
OF REFUGE

ALSO BY MARGARET PETERSON HADDIX

THE MISSING SERIES
Found
Sent
Sabotaged
Torn
Caught
Risked
Revealed
Redeemed

THE SHADOW CHILDREN
Among the Hidden
Among the Impostors
Among the Betrayed
Among the Barons
Among the Brave
Among the Enemy
Among the Free

THE PALACE CHRONICLES
Just Ella
Palace of Mirrors
Palace of Lies

UNDER THEIR SKIN SERIES
Under Their Skin
In Over Their Heads

CHILDREN OF EXILE SERIES
Children of Exile
Children of Refuge
Children of Jubilee

The Girl with 500 Middle Names
Because of Anya
Say What?
Dexter the Tough
Running Out of Time
Full Ride
Game Changer
The Always War
Claim to Fame
Uprising
Double Identity
The House on the Gulf
Escape from Memory
Takeoffs and Landings
Turnabout
Leaving Fishers
*Don't You Dare Read This,
Mrs. Dunphrey*

The Summer of Broken Things

CHILDREN OF EXILE:
BOOK 2

CHILDREN OF REFUGE

MARGARET PETERSON HADDIX

SIMON & SCHUSTER BOOKS FOR YOUNG READERS

NEW YORK LONDON TORONTO SYDNEY NEW DELHI

SIMON & SCHUSTER BOOKS FOR YOUNG READERS

An imprint of Simon & Schuster Children's Publishing Division

1230 Avenue of the Americas, New York, New York 10020

This book is a work of fiction. Any references to historical events, real people, or real places are used fictitiously. Other names, characters, places, and events are products of the author's imagination, and any resemblance to actual events or places or persons, living or dead, is entirely coincidental.

Text copyright © 2017 by Margaret Peterson Haddix

Cover illustration copyright © 2017 by Aaron Goodman

SIMON & SCHUSTER BOOKS FOR YOUNG READERS is a trademark of Simon & Schuster, Inc.

For information about special discounts for bulk purchases, please contact

Simon & Schuster Special Sales at 1-866-506-1949 or business@simonandschuster.com.

The Simon & Schuster Speakers Bureau can bring authors to your live event.

For more information or to book an event, contact the Simon & Schuster Speakers Bureau

at 1-866-248-3049 or visit our website at www.simonspeakers.com.

Also available in a Simon & Schuster Books for Young Readers hardcover edition

Book design by Krista Vossen

The text for this book was set in Weiss Std.

Manufactured in the United States of America

1018 OFF

First Simon & Schuster Books for Young Readers paperback edition November 2018

2 4 6 8 10 9 7 5 3 1

The Library of Congress has cataloged the hardcover edition as follows:

Names: Haddix, Margaret Peterson, author.

Title: Children of refuge / Margaret Peterson Haddix.

Description: First edition. | New York : Simon & Schuster Books for Young Readers, [2017]

| Series: Children of exile ; 2 |

Summary: Many surprises await twelve-year-old Edwy Watanaboneset when the Freds return him to Cursed Town, including that he has siblings in Refuge City who he will join in boarding school.

Identifiers: LCCN 2016028252| ISBN 9781442450066 (hardcover) | ISBN 9781442450080 (eBook)

| ISBN 9781442450073 (pbk)

Subjects: | CYAC: Brothers and sisters—Fiction. | Boarding schools—Fiction. | Schools—Fiction.

| Adventure and adventurers—Fiction. | Extraterrestrial beings—Fiction. | Science fiction.

Classification: LCC PZ7.H1164 Chj 2017 | DDC [Fic]—dc23

LC record available at https://lccn.loc.gov/2016028252

For all the Edwys in the world

CHILDREN OF REFUGE

PROLOGUE

The man lunged out of the darkness to grab me as I ran by.

"Let go!" I screamed, struggling to break away. "Let! Me! Go!"

I was already being chased by a pack of angry men. It didn't seem fair that someone I hadn't even seen was after me too.

Of course, my friend Rosi had told me once that I had a talent for making people mad.

Rosi . . .

She'd been running from the angry men too. Had she at least managed to get away safely?

I glanced over my shoulder, as if there was some way to see through the darkness and multiple rows of houses to make sure that she'd gotten back to her own home undetected. I'd been crashing through the trees and bushes beside the creek as loudly as possible, trying to get everyone to chase me, not her.

But I'd been counting on being able to run fast enough that no one caught up.

"Good," an oily voice whispered in my ear. "Now you understand that screaming is useless."

"No, I was just—" Before I could add *deciding what to scream next*, a thick hand slid over my mouth. It smelled like onions and sweat and mud and, I don't know, maybe puke as well.

Yes, definitely the puke part.

I bit down, my teeth sinking into the palm of the world's stinkiest hand.

The man jerked his hand back and muttered a few words I was pretty sure were swears. Having spent my first twelve years in Fredtown, the most boring place in the universe, I'd heard that there was such a thing as cursing, but had never been exposed to any actual curses. I'd left Fredtown only a few days ago, but those few days had been an education.

"Now you understand that holding on to me is useless," I said, which would have been a great last line before slipping away.

All hail the mighty Edwy Watanaboneset, escape artist extraordinaire, I thought.

But the man's right arm was like a chain around my middle. I squirmed and shoved, and the rocklike bulge of his muscles didn't budge.

Maybe I could be an escape artist extraordinaire only in

Fredtown, where the only people I'd ever had to escape were little kids and mild-mannered, unsuspecting Freds.

Maybe I'd have to outsmart this man instead.

"Do you know who I am?" I demanded. "Do you know who my parents are? Do you know what they'd do to anyone who hurt me?"

I was just finishing my first full day at "home"—back with the parents who gave birth to me, anyway, after the long overnight trip from Fredtown—but I'd already seen how everyone tiptoed around my parents. "Yes, Mr. Watanaboneset"; "As you wish, Mrs. Watanaboneset" . . . how many times had I heard someone speak those words? My parents *ruled*, in a way that would have horrified every single adult in Fredtown.

I could get used to that kind of power.

Except that my parents wanted to rule *me*, too.

"Yes, of course I know who you are," the man whispered in my ear. "You are a boy who will be killed if I hand you over to the men chasing you."

Killed?

I told myself he was just trying to scare me. Exaggerating wildly. But Rosi and I had been running away from a scary place neither of us understood, a scene of destruction where I was pretty sure people had died.

A long time ago.

Years in the past.

"I'm going to keep screaming," I told the man. "Everyone

3

will hear, and someone else will come running. Someone who works for my family, probably. And then *you* will be in trouble. You're the one who should worry about being killed."

The man clamped his hand back over my mouth, and this time he hooked his thumb over my nose and his pinky under my chin so I couldn't move my jaw. He slid his right arm up so that the crook of his elbow pressed painfully against my Adam's apple.

Back in Fredtown all the adults would faint dead away just at the thought of one person holding another person in that dangerous way. It felt like all the man would have to do was have a muscle spasm, and *that* could kill me.

"Before you say another word," the man hissed in my ear, "you might want to know who *I* am."

"Who is that?" I muttered, the words coming out as grunts, because he was holding my mouth shut and pressing so hard on my windpipe. But I could tell the man understood. He leaned his face even closer to my ear.

"I work for your father," the man said.

CHAPTER ONE

Nobody had told me that my parents' neighborhood was built on top of a secret tunnel up from the creek. So when the man dragged me into an innocuous-looking hole—and kept going and going and going—I instantly wanted to know more. We passed sputtering torches that seemed to throw off more shadows than light. The stench of the man's hand seemed to grow nastier and nastier. But we were deep underground before he finally eased his hand off my mouth and nose and jaw and I could manage more than grunts.

"What do you mean, you work for my father?" I asked. "Do you mean you *used* to work for him, but now you're betraying him by kidnapping his son? Why did you grab me? Where are you taking me? Where does this tunnel lead? How many people know about it?"

Six questions in practically a single breath. I thought that was pretty good considering he'd been restricting my oxygen supply for at least the past ten minutes.

I inhaled deeply and instantly thought of a dozen more questions I wanted to ask. But coming home had taught me that adults who weren't Freds sometimes reacted badly to questions. And this man definitely wasn't a peace-loving Fred. Even though he'd stopped acting like he was going to choke or gag me, he'd only shifted the pressure. He wrapped his muscular right arm around my waist again, and he quickly twisted his left arm and hand around to grab and immobilize my hands and feet simultaneously—a neat trick I wanted to figure out how to do myself. The way he was holding me, it kind of felt like he could snap any number of my bones as casually as someone else might shoo away a fly. I decided to wait for a moment and see if he'd answer any of the questions I'd already asked.

He grunted.

"Only way anyone leaves your father's employment is in a casket," he said. "*He* told me to grab you. And this tunnel leads to his secret underground office. That's where we're going now. To see him."

The tunnel curved slightly to the left, and I tried to calculate distances and angles in the near-total darkness. We were going in the direction of my parents' house, but how far belowground were we?

"Is there some secret stairway down from my house to this tunnel?" I asked. "Why didn't my parents tell me? It would have been a much better way for me to sneak out tonight."

The man did nothing but grunt this time, but it was a disapproving grunt, an annoyed grunt. I had a lifetime of experience irritating adults, but back in Fredtown the adults always tried to hide how much I bothered them. Which was weird, since they were always telling us kids we needed to get in touch with our feelings.

The sporadic lineup of torches on the wall ended, and I could see nothing but darkness ahead. The man was holding me at an angle that prevented me from seeing his face, so I had no warning when he lifted me just enough that he could stab his right elbow repeatedly against the wall—entering some kind of code, maybe?

There was a clanking sound, like a garage door opening. Could garage doors be reinforced? Coated with armor? Whatever it was, it sounded heavy.

The man took five steps forward into the darkness and jabbed his elbow against the wall again. Suddenly electric lights glowed in front of us, a row of single bulbs nestled at even intervals along the rock walls. The clanking sound happened again too. I glanced back and saw a scarred sheet of metal descending from the ceiling behind me. It slammed against the ground, cutting us off from the portion of the tunnel we'd just walked through.

"Are you getting tired of carrying me?" I asked the man.

"You can put me down now. You know even if I wanted to escape, I couldn't get out. Because of that door."

"I follow your father's orders," the man snarled.

"Do you pick your nose if my father tells you to pick your nose?" I asked. "Would you eat the booger if he said to?"

Okay, I knew that was kind of childish—the Freds said I should have outgrown booger jokes by the time of my twelfth birthday, which was six months ago. But if I wasn't very mature, it was their fault for raising me in a place where, besides Rosi, every other kid I knew was younger than me. When we could get away from the Freds, all my friends loved booger jokes.

Well, unless you counted Rosi as one of my friends. Which I had kind of started doing again.

The man carrying me didn't scold, but he didn't laugh, either.

"I follow your father's orders," he repeated, and squeezed a little harder against my ribs.

If I were goody-goody, well-behaved, *perfect* Rosi instead of my usual grown-up-defying, rude-joke-making, wouldn't-be-serious self, could I have won this man over? Could I have gotten him to put me down?

It was starting to scare me that he was holding on so tight.

My mind flashed back to Rosi again. I had convinced her to come out into the dangerous darkness with me because

I'd wanted to show her a vast area of burned-out, abandoned homes that puzzled me. I hadn't counted on men showing up there to meet in secret—men who chased after us when we accidentally made a noise. Surely there hadn't been yet another scary man waiting in the darkness to grab her, like there had been for me. The man clutching my ribs worked for my dad; it didn't seem likely that a similar man might work for her father. It didn't follow the rules of—what was it the Freds were always trying to teach me? Oh yeah: logic.

And Rosi had to have gotten away from the scary men who were chasing us, because I was making all the noise, and she was creeping away in silence. Rosi was so much better at being quiet than I was. She was better at everything the Freds valued.

The man carrying me stopped in front of a door. Even as he kept a firm grip on me, he rapped his knuckles against the door three times.

"Send him in." It was my father's voice, coming from an intercom speaker off to the side.

The door creaked open. In one smooth move the man dumped me on the floor, backed out, and then eased the door shut behind me.

I landed on the floor in a heap, my elbows tangled with my knees.

"Hey, hey, a little dignity here," I muttered.

At least this floor was carpeted, unlike the bare rock on the other side of the door. I unscrambled my arms and legs and rolled over onto my side, my face still pressed against the rug. I had a great view of dressy black shoes, polished to such a high sheen that I could practically see my face reflected in the toe tips.

I sat up, facing my father.

"What was that all about?" I demanded.

For a moment my father just stared at me. The Freds always said it didn't matter what you looked like, only what you did. Let's review:

Tonight my father ordered some guy who works for him to grab me, carry me down a dark tunnel, and drop me on the floor.

Earlier today my father punished me for asking questions.

Before yesterday I'd never seen my father in my life, unless maybe it was the day I was born. He never contacted me even once.

So, yeah. I wouldn't have given him a very good score on the doing.

But the way my dad looked? I hoped I would look like that when I grow up. He had this perfect bald head, his scalp so smooth you'd think his skin was made out of polished rock: Obsidian? Onyx? Jet stone? (Though maybe he wasn't actually bald. Maybe he just had his servants shave his head that perfectly every day. I hadn't been around him enough yet to know.) He could make his face look as hard as rock too. And he had this way of raising a single eyebrow that was just as intimidating as someone else flexing a muscle.

He did that now.

"You are not an obedient child," he said.

"Yeah, well, that's what the Freds always said," I told him.

I stood up, rubbing my right elbow where I'd banged it against the floor. Now at least I was more on my father's level, though I'd have to grow about a dozen centimeters to be able to look at him eye to eye, nose to nose, without tilting my head back. Back in Fredtown I'd been only a few centimeters away from being able to do that with my Fred-dad.

Curiosity got the better of me. It usually did.

"Have *you* ever met a Fred?" I asked my father. "What did you think of them? From what you saw of them, did you ever wonder—"

"Silence!" my father interrupted, slashing his hand through the air. "I talk; you listen. That's how this works."

It was *so* tempting to say, *Sure, if you answer my questions.* But my father's hand had cut so close to my face. And, though I was trying not to think about it, Rosi and I had been running away from a truly scary scene. And I didn't understand what the men who'd been chasing us wanted. And . . .

". . . for your safety," my father said.

"Wait, what?" I asked. "I zoned out a little bit there, and . . ."

"And that is exactly what I mean!" my father said, throwing his hands up in the air. "You don't listen! You don't obey! You ask questions you shouldn't ask!"

I felt a little proud. In just three seconds I'd reduced my father from All-Powerful Boss Who Can Make His Employees Do Anything He Wants to a weak man making the same helpless gesture my Fred-parents occasionally resorted to.

But my father wasn't finished talking.

"And that is why we are sending you to boarding school," he said.

CHAPTER TWO

I took a step back, my spine scraping against the solid wood of the door behind me. Boarding school? I'd never known anyone who'd gone to boarding school. Back in Fredtown, family was everything—even if it was just a fake family, with Fred-parents, not real ones. Freds wanted to spend every moment possible with their kids. As far as I knew, boarding schools only existed in stories, the kind the Freds read at bedtime from odd old books, the stories that began, *Once upon a time in a distant land . . .* Or *Long ago and far away . . .*

"But I just got here!" I protested. I was ashamed of how whiny I sounded, like the little kids leaving Fredtown just a couple of days ago crying, *But Fred-mommy! Fred-daddy! I don't want to leave! I love you!*

I hadn't had time to decide if I would ever love my real parents or not. I hadn't had time to know much of anything about them.

But maybe I knew enough.

I glanced quickly around my father's secret underground office, with its thick rugs and its enormous, gleaming desk. No joke—it had artwork enshrined under glass all along the walls. Expensive artwork, I'd guess.

"You're a smuggler and a thief," I said. "All the money you have is money you stole from someone else. The warehouse you have farther on in this tunnel? I bet it's full of stolen property. If—if you send me to boarding school, I'll tell everyone what you are. That you're a criminal."

I was guessing at half of that. Obviously I hadn't seen any warehouse. Yet. But my father's already rocklike face hardened.

"It doesn't matter," he said. "Nobody would believe you. You're just a kid."

I wondered if I'd taken the right tack. The Freds wouldn't have wanted me trying to blackmail and manipulate my father. They would have suggested some namby-pamby approach when I first saw other kids' luggage in my parents' house earlier today—the Freds would have wanted me to gently tell my father, *Don't you realize that when you take other people's property, it hurts them? Don't you know you always have to take other people's feelings into account? And have respect for their property rights, and all their other rights too?*

I'd returned Rosi's luggage to her immediately, along

with her younger brother Bobo's. I hadn't decided yet what to do about the other kids'.

But what I'd really wanted to do was ask my parents a lot more questions: *How does it work, stealing things? How do you get away with it? Aren't you scared that you'll be thrown into prison? Aren't you scared that, if people think they can get away with taking things that don't belong to them, then someone will take away something you want to keep?*

Oops. I think that last question might have sneaked in from a Fred lecture.

Questions weren't going to work now anyway. I'd started down the blackmail path; I needed to stick with it.

"*Someone* will believe me," I said. "I'm a good liar. Maybe I'll say *worse* things about you. I'll say you're the type of person who would hurt a kid."

Back in Fredtown, that was the worst crime anyone could commit.

My father's expression seemed to go up a few notches on the Mohs' hardness scale. Hadn't Rosi and I learned in science class that diamond was the hardest rock of all? If that was true, then my father's face had turned into black diamond.

"Your mother and I are sending you away for your own good," he said. "She's so upset about it, she can't even bear to come down and say good-bye."

"She's barely spent twenty-four hours with me!" I protested, before I had time to think. "What does she care?"

Maybe my father's face wasn't quite black diamond. He winced.

"Nevertheless," he said.

He strode over to his desk and reached under it. I'd seen his desk upstairs in the house, in his nonsecret office. I'd seen where he had a button underneath it to call servants.

"Are you calling back the man who just dumped me on the floor?" I said. "Really? You're going to put me in the care of a man who would *threaten* me? I guess *you* told him to kidnap me, but do you know he said he might hand me over to people who would *kill* me?"

"I trust Udans to get you out of this town and safely on to the boarding school in Refuge City," my father said. But he hesitated.

"Refuge City? Huh?" I asked. "Where's that? And what happens when I get there? I'm twelve years old! You trust this Udans guy to *raise* me? Udans and some *boarding* school . . . Would you and my mother even come to visit? Would I even have a family anymore? Every kid needs a family!"

Sometimes I couldn't help it, and something really, really Fred-like came out of my mouth.

Rosi said her parents punished her for sounding like a Fred. But my father just bit his lip.

"Unfortunately, your mother and I will not be able to visit," he said. "But you *will* have family with you at boarding school. You'll have your brother and sister."

"What are you talking about?" I asked. "Do you know anything about me? I don't have a brother and sister! I'm an only child! I've always been an only child!"

"Is that what the Freds told you?" my father asked, and now his voice was hard too. "Is that something else they lied about?"

I waved my hands in the empty air before me, emphasizing that I was alone.

"Did you get any other kids back from Fredtown besides me?" I taunted. "Would you have noticed one way or another? Oh, that's right, you went twelve years without seeing your own kid, so maybe it's hard to remember if there's just one of me, or more!"

My father slumped into the chair behind the desk.

"Your brother and sister are both *older* than you," he said. "But . . ." The fierceness went out of his face and voice. "We haven't seen them in twelve years either. That's how long they've been in Refuge City."

CHAPTER THREE

For the first time in my life, I was actually speechless. I was pretty sure my parents hadn't been allowed to visit me in Fredtown. But why would they have two other kids someplace else that they also hadn't bothered visiting?

How could I have a brother and sister I didn't even know?

How could I be the *youngest* kid in my family?

What kind of family was scattered in three different places?

My father held up his hands like he could tell I had almost recovered my powers of speech and was about to unleash a barrage of questions.

"I thought there'd be time to explain everything," my father said. "Later. Once you . . . trusted us a little more."

I was so stunned by his words I almost fell down to the floor again. He wanted to explain *everything*? Wasn't he like the Freds, who always told me I wasn't old enough to know any of the things I really wanted to know?

Did my father think I was already old enough? Why was I old enough tonight, when I hadn't been old enough earlier today?

How could he think I would ever trust him?

Somehow I managed to keep standing. Somehow I managed to take five steps forward and grab my father's arm, holding him back from pressing the button under his desk.

"Explain now," I said. "If I really do have a brother and sister . . . why did you send them away twelve years ago? Why didn't you send me with them, before the Freds got me? Why—"

"There was a war," my father said.

I looked at him blankly. I vaguely recognized the word "war" from some history class back in Fredtown. But Rosi was the one who paid attention in history class. Not me. I think our teacher had been talking about war that time Rosi said afterward, walking home, "Edwy, you should have listened today. *You* would have enjoyed hearing about people fighting. You would have liked finding out all the horrible things people did, before they became civilized. You would have thought it was exciting."

Did war have something to do with fighting?

No way the Freds would have taught us anything about fighting. The only reason I even knew the word "fighting" was because it was on their long list of things we weren't allowed to do.

"You mean, in ancient times," I said to my father. "There was war a long time ago."

My father gave a barking laugh. It kind of hurt to hear.

"I suppose to a twelve-year-old, twelve years ago is ancient times," he said bitterly. "The war happened *only* twelve years ago. When it started, we sent your brother and sister, Enu and Kiandra, to Refuge City to keep them safe. You weren't born yet. Not until the day the war ended. And that was the day the Freds started taking babies away."

It was like he was handing me puzzle pieces that didn't fit right into the huge, gaping holes in my knowledge. *This* wasn't what I wanted to know. Or was it?

I remembered the scary scene Rosi and I had been running away from: the vast area of burned houses, destroyed homes. Was that the kind of thing that happened during war? From fighting?

I couldn't imagine it. My father had to be lying.

But before I could say so, a box on my father's desk crackled.

"Guard location one, reporting in," a voice said. I guess the box was an intercom. "The enemy has dispersed. Cloud cover is heavy. This is prime go time."

"Understood," my father said.

His arm jerked out of my grasp. I could tell: He'd pressed the button under his desk.

The door swung open.

"I won't go anywhere," I said. "I'll scream. I'll run away. I'll fight."

My father lurched forward and held me tight . . .

. . . just long enough for Udans to tie my hands together, jerk a blindfold over my eyes, and shove a gag into my mouth.

And then Udans carried me out the door.

CHAPTER FOUR

I struggled against Udans's grip, but it was useless. I was like a bug caught in a spider's web, a mouse under a cat's paw—immobilized. (And why had the gentle Freds let us learn about bugs and mice, creatures that were doomed to die? What were they thinking? Why hadn't they taught us more about war? Or . . . about how to fight back when someone kidnaps you?)

"You're only making it worse for yourself," Udans muttered as he kept striding forward.

And then he put me down. He didn't bend over—it felt more like he'd laid me on a table or in some sort of cupboard roughly at the level of his waist.

"It's a long drive," Udans said. "It'd be easiest if you just slept."

Drive? I thought. Had he just put me in a car or a truck? I rolled side to side and stretched out my legs, feeling for the dimensions of the compartment I was in. It wasn't upholstered, like the seat of a car would be. It was more like a box.

"There's food and water beside your head," Udans added. "You can figure out how to reach it. I wouldn't recommend spilling anything."

And then I heard a clanking sound above me, as if he'd sealed off the top of my box. I twisted around, reached up my bound hands—and, yes, a plank of solid wood lay just centimeters above my face.

The box I was in? It was about the size of a coffin.

"No, wait—what if I'm claustrophobic?" I tried to yell up to Udans. I didn't think I was, but he didn't have to know that. "This is wrong! It's not fair!"

Thanks to the gag on my mouth, my words came out as gibberish. It probably didn't matter, because I heard receding footsteps—Udans walking away from me?—and then the roar of an engine.

Truck engine, not car, I decided, based on the intensity of the sputtering rattle. *And in need of a tune-up.*

Rosi and I had had a course in basic auto mechanics last school year, and that was one subject I had paid attention to.

The truck lurched forward, and I slid toward the back wall of my box. I didn't know how long Udans intended to keep me here—his "long drive" didn't sound promising—but I had no intention of rolling back and forth and slamming into walls every time he stopped and started. I curled my hands back and started picking at the knots binding my wrists together.

"I *am* an amazing escape artist," I muttered to myself.

Either that was true, or Udans had not actually intended to keep me gagged and blindfolded and bound for much longer than it took to stash me in this box. The knots weren't that tight, and I freed myself quickly. As soon as I had my hands free, I shoved against the wood plank at the top of the box, but it didn't budge.

You are not claustrophobic. You are not claustrophobic, I told myself.

But, really, how would I know? That was the kind of thing the Freds would never have let us test out, back in Fredtown. This box was the smallest confined space I'd ever been in.

So what? You can take it! You're Edwy Watanaboneset!

Edwy Watanaboneset, whose own father had just had him kidnapped and sent away. Who was going to be stuck going to boarding school in some strange place called Refuge City if he didn't find a way out.

You always think of a way out, I told myself.

I imagined the admiring looks of the cluster of younger kids who often followed me around back in Fredtown. They'd be so impressed if they ever heard about my escaping this. I could recast the whole story of this night to make myself into quite the hero. Okay, I might have to lie a little, but still. . . .

Somehow the awed little-kid faces I was trying to

imagine got pushed aside in my brain. Instead what I pictured was Rosi's face, Rosi telling me, as only she could, *Edwy, be careful! Not everything's a joke, you know! I don't want you to get hurt!*

It was strange. Those were almost exactly the words a Fred would use. I could easily have imagined my Fred-teachers, Fred-mama, or Fred-daddy saying those things. Maybe even my real mother, too, if it was true that she was too worried about me to say good-bye. If she actually, you know, cared. But it felt different to imagine Rosi worrying about me.

Wouldn't Rosi laugh, to know that I actually have *feelings,* I told myself.

But thinking about Rosi calmed me down. It kept me from banging my fists on the wood plank above my head, or screaming and screaming and screaming—uselessly, because any sound I made would surely get lost in the rattle of the engine noise.

Udans gave me food and water, I reminded myself. *He doesn't intend for me to die in here. I can probably even pee in an empty water bottle, if I have to. So I'm taken care of. I just . . . have to be ready to jump up and run away when he stops the car and opens this box. This coffin.*

I braced my legs against the side of my box. I *was* ready. Edwy the Amazing was prepared.

CHAPTER FIVE

It's really hard to stay braced and ready for hours on end, you know?

I had no way of keeping track of how much time passed, but the truck's engine was a steady rumble for what felt like hours. After a while I got hungry and ate some of the food stashed above my head—grapes and a tasty chicken sandwich and sweet clumps of what might have been cookies made of rice. The food distracted me from the rotting stench that still seemed to linger in my nose, from when Udans held his hand over my face for so long. The only thing available to drink was a huge bottle of water—so boring—but at least it kept me from staying thirsty. And you try gulping down any sort of beverage while lying in a shallow box and being jolted back and forth constantly. The water kind of doubled as a drink and a shower.

After I'd eaten all the food I could lay my hands on, I rolled onto my side and imagined how I'd swing my arms out as soon as I saw the first crack of light above me. Everybody said I'd been the strongest kid in Fredtown; surely as soon as Udans unlatched the plank above me, I'd be able to sweep the plank aside, shove past him, and take off.

The truck's engine kept humming along. The darkness around me stayed constant. Unending.

I don't remember closing my eyes, but I was sound asleep when a bright light suddenly washed over me. I wasted a moment wincing and blinking, and then I could see Udans standing above me, a dark shadow in the glare of bright sunlight behind him. He had removed the plank entirely, exposing me to the world outside the truck.

And the truck was stopped.

I sprang up and took off running. My feet touched the flat surface of the truck's bed only once before I leaped down to the ground. I hit with such force that I had to crouch for an instant and touch my fingertips to the road to balance, but then I was back up, sprinting away. There wasn't even time to look where I was going—I was all about *speed*.

I raced forward, stretching my legs out as far as I could, shoving off from every step with my full strength. But Udans was taller than me, and stronger, too. Was he a faster runner as well? How much time did I have before he caught up with me? How many seconds did I have before I'd need to shout for help, or to find a way to outsmart him and hide?

I risked a glance over my shoulder, even as I kept running blindly forward.

Udans was still back at the truck, leaning against the bumper. He wasn't even chasing me.

"Run all you like," he said with a yawn. "Let me know when you get tired."

"You can't catch me!" I yelled back. "When my dad finds out I've escaped, he'll . . ."

I finally noticed the scenery around me. Forget yelling for help—there was no one around besides me and Udans. Forget hiding—there was nothing in sight but Udans, the truck, and hectare after hectare of flat, scrubby land. The tallest plant I could see barely came up to my ankles. The ground was hard and dusty and cracked, as if eons had passed since the last time it rained. And this drought-stricken wasteland stretched all the way to the horizon.

I could run all I liked. But there was nowhere to run to.

There was nowhere for me to go.

CHAPTER SIX

My running flagged.

"Done?" Udans said, stifling another yawn. "Figured out yet that you'll die of thirst and starvation if you don't come back to this truck? Or . . . if you wait to come back until after I decide to leave?"

Something like panic rose up in the back of my throat—or maybe the chicken sandwich I'd eaten had gone bad and wanted to claw its way back out. But I couldn't let Udans see that he'd beaten me.

And how could I go back to that truck without admitting defeat? Without losing face?

If Udans were a Fred, he'd have left me an easy way out, a way to avoid any shame, I thought. *Instead of rubbing it in my face that he's right and I just made a fool of myself. . . .*

I'd always hated it when the Freds did their fake little routines of pretending, *Oh, look! Everyone's a winner!* As if I couldn't tell that they were really saying, *As long as you do what* we *want . . .*

But how was I supposed to give in when Udans hadn't given me an easy way to do that?

I slowed my pace to a shuffle, but I kept moving farther and farther from the truck.

"Oh, kid, don't be like that," Udans said, shaking his head and rolling his eyes. "Would it help if I told you I came to get you so you could ride up front with me? Now that we're past the border?"

I stopped.

"Why didn't you say that before?" I said stiffly.

"Did you give me time?" Udans asked. He stood up and brushed dust off his canvas pants, from where he'd leaned on the bumper. "Come on. I've got soda pop on ice up in the cab."

Did he think I could be bribed?

Well, okay, I probably could be.

"You answer questions, too," I said stubbornly. "Then it's a deal. What do you mean, 'past the border'? Why did I have to hide before, but I don't have to now? What border are you talking about? Why's there a border? What is this Refuge City place, anyway?"

Udans winced, as if my questions hurt his ears.

"Kid, you're going to make me reconsider," he groaned.

I was glad he said that. Now I could defy him by doing what I wanted anyhow. I dashed back to the truck, swung open the door to the passenger side, and scrambled in.

"Too late," I called back to Udans. I hung my head out the window like a dog. "I'm already here."

I was betting it would take too much effort for him to come around to my side of the truck, yank me out of my seat, and deal with me kicking and screaming while he tried to stuff me back into my hiding place in the rear of the truck.

And I was right. Udans just sighed once. Then he walked around the truck, slid into the driver's seat, and turned the key.

CHAPTER SEVEN

The scrubby, dry, flat landscape looked a lot better whizzing by at more than a hundred kilometers an hour while I sat in the cab of the truck gulping down a fizzy grape-flavored drink. I decided maybe I should be nice to Udans—or at least strategic about the best way to get him to answer my questions. So for a few minutes I just gazed around, taking everything in.

The sun was high overhead now, so I guessed I'd been in my hiding place all night and then late into the morning. We had to be hours away from my parents and their hometown.

The truck cab was dusty from having the windows open, but otherwise it was pretty tidy. Which maybe meant that Udans was as much of an annoying neatnik as my Fred-parents. A thick cooler sat between Udans and me, and when he'd opened it to give me the grape drink, I'd seen that it was well stocked (which I appreciated) and well organized (which I didn't).

The road ahead of us was unpaved, just a dusty set of tire tracks leading toward . . .

Oh, wait, it's not just flat, dry land everywhere, I realized. *There's a mountain up ahead! Is that where we're going? Is Refuge City in the mountains?*

I opened my mouth to ask Udans those questions. Then I looked at his face—really looked.

The whole time I lived in Fredtown, I'd never thought that much about how all the grown-ups—the Freds—always had pleasant expressions on their faces. I mean, it drove me crazy how many times they said things like, *Oh, Edwy, we are disappointed in your behavior, but you know we always love you, don't you? Even though you dyed the dog's fur blue. Even though you didn't do your homework. Even though . . .*

Well. No need to list everything I ever did wrong in Fredtown.

What I never thought about was that all those times, the Freds' faces really did look like they loved me, no matter what. They always gazed at me so kindly, their eyes so wide and sympathetic, their expressions so annoyingly gentle. . . . It was always a little hard not to feel sorry about what I'd done.

The first time I ever saw an adult with a mean expression on his face was the day all of us Fredtown kids got on the plane to go back to our real parents' hometown. The men on the plane—they *glared*. They snarled. They slammed a door in Rosi's face.

And even though I'd maybe been known to slam a door

in Rosi's face once or twice myself, to have an adult do that seemed unbelievable.

Unfair.

Totally wrong.

Then we all got to our parents' hometown, and lots of people there looked mean or angry or nasty or upset.

Cruelty looks a lot scarier on an adult's face than on a kid's, you know?

That is, if I even understood things right. It was like there was some secret code I'd missed learning, because I'd grown up in Fredtown: See the downward slope of an eyebrow—oh, that person's mad. See the curl of a lip—that person's ready to say something mean. See the sneering wrinkling up of a nose—is it possible that that person hates you?

Maybe none of us kids had ever looked that mean or angry or nasty or upset back in Fredtown. Maybe it was too late for me to really learn the code.

Last night Udans had looked mean, in the few glimpses I'd gotten of his face. He'd *been* mean, grabbing me and stuffing me into the secret compartment in the back of the truck.

Today he'd let me out of that horrid claustrophobic box. But his face stayed twisted. Was it just because he had a little scar on his right cheek, a small X pulling his skin back toward his ear? Was it just because he was squinting into the bright sunlight?

Or was he mean? Did I need to be on guard the entire time I spent with him?

Last night all I'd really noticed about Udans was that he had a lot of muscles. Now I took in the fact that he was really tall—the top of his head bumped up against the roof of the truck cab. And, even with the scar—maybe *because* of the scar—he looked really cool. With his hair pulled back into a little tail at the base of his neck, he looked like a pirate from one of those storybooks we had back in Fredtown.

The pirates in those storybooks only ever *pretended* to be bad.

I decided maybe Udans was like that too. I decided maybe I could trust him. For now.

"About that border you were talking about . . . ," I said over the roar of the air coming in the windows.

I hoped Udans appreciated that I wasn't spitting twenty-seven questions at him at once, like I really wanted to.

Udans glanced toward me, tilted his head as if considering, then started rolling up his window.

"Roll yours up too, and we can turn on the air-conditioning, so I don't have to shout to be heard," he said.

I didn't have to be asked twice. By the time I had my window up, the truck cab was a lot quieter, and we had cool air blasting at us from the dashboard.

"Your father says I should know that not every boss lets his employees use a truck with air-conditioning," Udans said. "He says I should appreciate his generosity."

"Is that true?" I asked. "*Is* it generosity?"

Udans grinned, like I'd passed some test.

"Between you and me, I think he just happened to steal a truck with air-conditioning," Udans said.

Once again I wanted to know how my father got away with stealing things. But Udans was wincing again.

"So," he began. "You want to know about the border. Your father really should have told you."

"Maybe he thought you'd do a better job of telling," I said, as smarmy as any Fred I'd ever met.

Udans reached across the cooler between us and punched me in the arm.

"Oh, it's going to be like that?" he asked. "You really *are* the old man's son."

Was he saying I was like my dad?

"The border . . . ," I prompted Udans again.

"You know about the war?" he asked.

I nodded, pretending I knew everything.

"During the war, the countries around us sealed off their borders from us, so the fighting wouldn't spill over into their lands," Udans said. His voice was thick with bitterness. "They didn't care what happened to *us*, as long as it didn't hurt *them*."

"But my father told me the war ended," I said. "Twelve years ago. The day I was born."

Udans shot me a glance I didn't understand.

"Yeah, well, the borders stayed closed," he said. "Our neighbors still don't trust us. Because of our history. The only ones allowed in or out, past the border, are people like me, delivering supplies. *That's* why I had to smuggle you across, hidden under a vat of our nation's smelliest cheeses. The border guards never want to touch those."

Maybe that explained why Udans's hand on my mouth had smelled like puke last night. Maybe that explained why I'd kept smelling that odor, down in the secret compartment.

Udans was watching me too carefully, his eyes steady on my face, not on the road ahead. Had I missed something?

Suddenly I understood. Or thought I did.

"Wait a minute, are you saying my parents and . . . and everyone else in their town . . . it's like they're prisoners?" I asked. "They're trapped forever?"

It wasn't really my parents I was worried about. It was Rosi.

Udans nodded.

I reached out and grabbed the steering wheel, yanking it as far as I could to the right.

CHAPTER EIGHT

"**What the—?**"

Udans shoved my hand away from the steering wheel so fast and so hard that my whole body slammed against the door. He jerked the steering wheel back to the left, so the truck did nothing more than wobble, rather than spin around in the opposite direction the way I'd intended.

"Are you completely *nuts*?" he asked. He let out a stream of words under his breath that I was certain had to be curses. "And here I thought your old man was the crazy one. . . ."

"Turn around!" I yelled at him. "We've got to rescue—"

"Oh, *now* you choose to become the loyal son, who wants to rescue his parents?" Udans hollered at me. "Now, when you could have flipped the truck and killed us both?"

I really hadn't thought about that before I'd grabbed the steering wheel. I really hadn't thought much at all before I'd acted.

The Freds always told me I had a problem with that.

"There's no way anyone could smuggle *adults* into Refuge City," Udans went on. "There's too much red tape, too much paperwork. . . . But don't feel too bad for your parents. Did you see the size of their house? Did you see how many cars they have parked in their driveway? They might as well be king and queen of the restricted zone. Your father pretty much *is* the king. The crime king, anyway."

I'd had twelve years of Fred lectures about how material goods didn't really matter that much, once you had your basic needs. Was that why I kept seeing my father's face in my mind, how sad he'd looked when he said he hadn't seen my brother and sister in twelve years?

"Don't worry, kid," Udans said, as if I were the one looking sad. "The forged papers your father bought are good enough to get *you* into Refuge City."

He patted the pocket of his shirt, as if he had all the papers stowed there.

I swallowed hard.

"What about . . . the other kids?" I asked. I wasn't going to say Rosi's name. "There were a lot of us who came back from Fredtown. What if some of them are my friends? What if I want to get them out?"

"You think *you* could . . . ? Not possible," Udans said with a shrug. "But don't worry. I'm sure you'll make new friends in Refuge City. That's just how life goes. There's nothing you can do about it."

I gaped at him. *That's just how life goes? There's nothing you can do?* Who said stuff like that? Who would believe it?

That was pretty much the anti-Fred philosophy. The Freds were all about, *You can make a difference! You can change the world! You can always help your friends! You have a moral obligation to take care of the people around you!*

I mean, I'd tried really, really hard *not* to memorize all their namby-pamby precepts and founding principles and words to live by. But except for the past few days, I'd spent my whole life in Fredtown. Their stupid sayings were stuck in my brain like bugs on flypaper.

"If my friends wanted to get forged papers of their own . . . ," I tried again. I could imagine sending a letter or something back to Rosi, telling her what to do.

"They'd better have rich parents of their own," Udans said. "Parents every bit as rich as your dad."

He might as well have added: *And nobody else back in your hometown is that rich.*

I'd seen where Rosi's family lived. It was pretty much a plywood box with a corrugated tin roof.

They weren't rich. They were probably just happy not to be the poorest people in town.

"Maybe my parents could pay for—" I began.

Udans cracked up.

"Oh, that's a good one!" He laughed so hard I was a little afraid he'd drive off the road. "You really think your dad would pay for someone else? Instead of getting more money for himself? *How* much time did you spend with your father?"

Enough, I thought.

I slumped against the door. The grape-soda taste left over in my mouth seemed too sweet now. It tasted almost as bad as Udans's hand had smelled last night.

"Hey, hey—don't be like that!" Udans said. "You are going to love it in Refuge City. Everyone does. The lights, the food, the tall buildings, the parks . . . it's the best place ever."

"So why don't you just stay there all the time?" I muttered.

"You think *I* have the right authorization to live permanently in Refuge City?" Udans asked with a snort. "If only I did! I could do without this drive twice a week. I could do without . . ." He turned his squint from the road to me. "Oh, never mind."

"Never mind what?" I asked suspiciously.

"Never mind me," Udans said smoothly. "Just think about how lucky you are to be going to Refuge City!"

I didn't feel lucky. I felt . . . sad. Like I missed Rosi. Which was crazy, because for probably half the time we'd ever spent together, either she was mad at me or I was mad at her.

But I don't know if she got home safely last night. I don't know if anyone lunged at her and grabbed her out of the darkness. I don't know if she's okay.

I stared out the windshield, the dry, dead land rushing toward me.

"So did you run out of questions?" Udans finally asked, in a way that made me think maybe I'd been staring out the windshield thinking about nothing for a very, very long time.

Besides the ones about Rosi, you mean? I wondered.

I did have a lot of other questions: What had the war been like? What did that really mean, that there'd been a war? Had people actually fought? What had my parents done, when there was fighting going on? Why had my parents decided to send me away so quickly after I'd just gotten home? Why had the Freds taken all the other kids and me away from our parents in the first place? Did it have anything to do with the war? Why had we been sent back home? Why hadn't my brother and sister been sent home at the same time? How could I ever learn how to deal with mean people—or just people who said, *There's nothing you can do*, when the Freds had always said there was always something you could do?

What if there really was nothing I could do to help Rosi?

Or what if there was, and I was too much of a coward to do it?

All those questions led back to Rosi somehow. So I couldn't ask any of them.

I sighed and came up with a question for Udans. A safe one. One I didn't even care about.

"When was the last time you gave this truck's engine a tune-up?" I asked.

CHAPTER NINE

Refuge City glittered.

Udans pointed out the glow on the horizon while we were still far, far away. Then as we got closer, he started naming landmarks: "Oh, look, there's the Crystal Tower. . . . See those five domes at the foot of the mountain? That's a sports complex, the Athletic Zone—people call it the AZ. Or sometimes the Azzz. There's always some game to watch or play there, day or night. . . . When the road turns to the right in a little bit you can see straight down the Gulch—that's the biggest row of skyscrapers. . . . Last I heard, Refuge City had seventy buildings taller than seventy stories. . . . People made a big deal about the matching numbers, but I think there are even more now. . . ."

Just being close to Refuge City made him talk more, sit up straighter, drive faster.

In spite of myself I felt a jolt of excitement, of anticipation. Refuge City looked like the kind of place I'd dreamed of, back in dreary little Fredtown. I remembered that first meeting in Fredtown when the Freds had said, *You're all going home,* and the little kids had started asking about playgrounds and toys and everything they didn't want to leave behind. I'd mostly thought about what lay ahead: I'd pictured towers and skyscrapers and sports domes, scenes from big, exciting cities I'd only read about. I'd wanted that, even if I hadn't trusted the Freds to give it to me.

Maybe Refuge City was the type of place I really belonged.

Maybe I was being silly worrying about Rosi. The Freds *loved* her; they never disapproved of anything about her. If she was in any actual danger, back in our hometown, they'd swoop in and take care of her. It really wasn't all up to me.

"Is my boarding school in one of those skyscrapers?" I asked. Fredtown hadn't had any buildings taller than three stories, and the only elevator I'd ever been in was at the town hall. (For some reason, my Fred-parents almost always wanted me to use up as much energy as possible by taking the stairs.) It wasn't like the town-hall elevator was that big of a treat, anyway: You could fall asleep waiting for it to go from the first to the second floor. But if Refuge City had buildings that were more than seventy stories tall, wouldn't they have really fast elevators? Elevators that were as cool as amusement-park rides?

"Your school? Er . . . no," Udans said. "It's not in a sky-scraper."

"Then could I—"

"You know what? I've got to focus on driving right now," Udans said. "Save your questions for your brother and sister, when you meet them. Yes, that's it. They can answer your questions."

My stomach lurched, but it couldn't have been because I was nervous about meeting my brother and sister. It was prob-ably just because Udans jerked the steering wheel abruptly to the right, to avoid a tiny convertible that had darted past his front tires like a bug trying to zip past a bull.

We were on the outskirts of the city now, and all the traf-fic around us swooped and zoomed over hills, around curves, and into and out of tunnels. Udans's truck had seemed so impressive out in the wilderness—it had air-conditioning and everything! But now it couldn't seem to keep up. It suddenly seemed old and old-fashioned with so many sleek, gleaming cars around us.

A shiny red sports car cut us off, and Udans had to drive up onto the curb to avoid it, before lumbering back onto the street.

"Are we almost there?" I asked. "To the school, I mean? Or . . . where my brother and sister live?"

"It's not too far," Udans said.

But then we rounded a corner, and the road ahead looked

like a parking lot, every car and truck at a standstill.

"I thought they'd finished the construction here. . . . Ugh," Udans muttered.

I opened my mouth to suggest changing lanes, but I got distracted because the red sports car in front of us suddenly revved its engine, as if the driver thought he'd still be able to keep speeding forward. Maybe even straight through the semitruck in front of him.

"Is he crazy? There's nowhere to go! He's going to crash—" I began.

The car did zoom forward—and upward. It launched right up into the airspace *above* the semi. And then, while I watched, the sports car zipped out of sight, high over every stopped truck and car.

"Sweet!" I cried.

I knew there were such things as flying cars, but I'd never seen one in real life. Back in Fredtown the Freds always said we had enough territory around us that we didn't need them—there was plenty of space for roads and highways down on the ground.

Here it's just an unnecessary risk, my Fred-dad always told me.

And then once I got to my parents' hometown, it had been pretty clear that everything there was even more primitive and backward.

"Why isn't *every* car and truck ahead of us doing that?" I asked Udans. "Why aren't *we*?"

He chuckled as if I'd said something funny.

"Do you know how expensive the fees are for the upper lanes?" he asked. "That's for billionaires only. And even your dad couldn't steal us a truck with hover capacity."

"I didn't see that guy pay any fee!" I protested, pointing after the vanished sports car. "He just . . ." I lifted my hand and zoomed it off toward the window, imitating.

Now Udans guffawed.

"Just because you don't see something doesn't mean it didn't happen," he said. "The minute that guy lifted off, the money came out of his bank account. Just like the minute we drove into Refuge City, the entry fee to the city came out of your dad's bank account. And your papers—and mine—were scanned electronically. Along with our genetic makeup."

Okay, that was a little scary.

"But how . . . ?" I began. I narrowed my eyes at Udans. "You're saying the papers were scanned through your shirt pocket? And our genetic makeup was scanned through our clothes and . . . and the truck windows? You're just pulling my leg, aren't you?"

Udans lifted his hands from the steering wheel, a gesture of innocence.

"It's true!" he said. "There are scanners and cameras

everywhere in Refuge City. See that little sparkly thing on that building?" He pointed to a brick structure off to the right. "I bet that's one. You just have to know where to look."

The "sparkly thing" he was pointing at might as well have been a fleck of silver glitter on one red brick.

I still thought Udans might be pulling my leg. But I acted cool, just in case.

"A city that can put scanners and cameras everywhere still lets people get stuck in traffic like this?" I taunted. "And there's not anything we can do about it?"

"Well, the two of us could get out and walk," Udans said. "We're close enough. It beats sitting here for the next hour."

"You'd just leave the truck here?" I asked, amazed.

"Not in the street—there'd be a big fee for that, too. But over there . . ."

It took him half an hour to maneuver out of traffic, but then he was able to park the truck in a lot behind a fueling station. I slipped out of the truck—and realized for the first time that I had no suitcase, no backpack, nothing but the clothes I was wearing. Which, now that I thought about it, were kind of ripped and muddy from my running along the edge of the creek last night.

"Um, my loving parents didn't tuck any of my belongings into your truck before they sent you out to kidnap me, did they?" I asked.

"They said you could buy new in Refuge City," Udans said. "I don't think they had a very high opinion of your old clothes."

I thought about the shirts and pants my Fred-parents had folded so neatly and placed so carefully into the suitcase they'd packed for me in Fredtown. There might have been a few places I'd torn out the knees of the pants a time or two, playing, but they'd been repaired.

Who cares about clothes? I told myself.

Actually, I did. New clothes were always too stiff and uncomfortable. My old clothes had been worn out just the right amount.

It wasn't that I was sentimental. It wasn't that I wouldn't know who I was in new clothes. It wasn't that everyone who'd ever really known me—like Rosi—had known me in my old clothes.

"I'm fine with new clothes," I told Udans.

For some reason my voice came out sounding fierce and bristly, as if I was saying something else entirely.

CHAPTER TEN

It should have felt good to stretch my legs after sitting in the truck for so long. But the sidewalks of Refuge City were crowded, and, oddly, I seemed to be the shortest person around. So my views tended to be of:

One man's or another's bulging belly, pressed uncomfortably close to my face;

A woman's purse, right before it clipped my ear;

Udans's back, which I tried to keep in sight at all times.

If I'd been, say, seven—or maybe even eight or nine—I wouldn't have been able to stop myself from whining, *Udans! Wait for me!* If I'd been even younger, I might have lost all dignity and begged, *Please! Let me hold your hand so I don't get lost!* But I was twelve, and I *was* Edwy the Amazing, Edwy the Awesome, the one all the little kids back in Fredtown had always looked up to.

So I darted around purses and bellies, and once or twice I even ducked under someone's elbow. I told myself Udans was probably glancing back over his shoulder all the time to make sure I was still with him. Just . . . not ever when I was looking.

Then came a moment when a woman in a towering hat— who seemed to have an entire garden growing on her head— stepped between Udans and me.

When I zipped around her, narrowly missing trouncing on the pointy toes of her red shoes, Udans had vanished.

I whipped my head back and forth, scanning the crowd ahead, catching glimpses of black-and-white checkered purses, men's shirts with gaping buttonholes, and then, when she stepped past me again, garden-hat lady. *She* didn't dodge *my* feet; her spiky heel stabbed right into the little-toe area of my right sneaker.

"Ow! Ow! Ow!" I jumped up and down, clutching my brutalized foot.

Garden-hat lady didn't even turn around.

But an arm darted out of a nearby doorway. I recognized Udans's bulging muscles and the sleeve of his dark gray T-shirt. He grabbed me and pulled me into the doorway.

"Did you see that?" I asked him. "Who *does* that? I think my toe's broken. Maybe even severed. Don't people here know not to walk on other people's feet?"

"Young man," Udans began. He crouched down, so he could speak directly into my ear, almost as if he were sharing a secret. "You are not the son of the richest man in Refuge City, the way you were the son of the richest man back in your hometown. You can't expect special treatment."

I jerked away from him.

"'Special treatment'?" I repeated. "Being able to walk around without anyone stepping on your toes should be, like, a basic right! No one deserves to have his toe speared like that. The Freds always said . . ."

I stopped myself because, yikes! Had I really been about to quote the Freds? They probably did have about fifty different founding principles that would apply to this situation—they usually had at least fifty different founding principles they tried to apply to *any* situation, and at one time or another, I'm sure, they'd quoted every single one at me. They could come up with fifty different reasons it was a bad idea to brush my teeth for two minutes and fifty-eight seconds instead of the full three minutes.

But *I* didn't quote Fred principles.

Also—Udans jerked back when I spoke the word "Freds," as if it frightened him.

When I stopped talking, he murmured, "That's right. It would be wise to say as little as possible about *them*."

This is how my brain works: I suddenly had the desire to run down the street yelling, "Freds! Freds! Freds! Freds! Freds!" just to see what happened.

But Udans's next words stopped me. He said:

"Anyhow, we're here. Are you ready to meet your brother and sister?"

CHAPTER ELEVEN

I forgot about my sore toe. I forgot the Freds and my weird desire to run around shouting about them. For a minute I might have even forgotten about Rosi.

"Um, sure," I told Udans. "Is this where they live? Is this where I'll live? Is this the school?"

Now that I knew this wasn't just some random doorway he'd pulled me into, I peeked past his shoulder, through a huge glass door. Beyond it was a sort of entryway—maybe it was a lobby?—that some artist might have thrown together and entitled *Chrome and Mirrors: Variations*. It was all so shiny, all so tricky with the mirrors throwing off dozens of versions of one another. I wondered how often the people who lived in this building walked into one of the mirrored walls thinking it was a way out.

"You'll see," Udans said, smiling cryptically.

I wanted to tell him that his cool-pirate act wasn't going to work on me, but he was already stepping through the door, and I was a little afraid I'd lose him again in all the mirrored reflections. Somehow he knew that there was a button hidden on one of the mirrors, and when he pressed it, a door slid open.

It was an elevator.

"Ooh, is this a skyscraper after all?" I asked, stepping in.

"Nope," Udans said, reaching past me for the control panel. The door closed behind us. "This building is only ten stories. But"—he grinned, and this time the smile was a little friendlier—"Enu and Kiandra *do* live on the top floor. The penthouse suite."

"Enu and Kiandra—that's my brother and sister?" I asked anxiously.

Those *were* the names my father had said, weren't they? Why hadn't I asked more about them sooner? Why hadn't I asked *everything* about them?

I knew why. I'd been too scared of meeting them. I'd mostly been avoiding thinking about them. Just like I was avoiding thinking about Rosi.

Udans nodded. And then—even though I hadn't felt the elevator moving—the door opened again, revealing shiny silver wallpaper ahead of us.

"This is the tenth floor?" I asked Udans. "Already?"

He laughed and nodded. I followed him out of the elevator. Only one door stood ahead of us, and he knocked on it.

"Use the doorbell!" a muffled voice yelled from behind the door.

"You know *I* never do that!" Udans growled back.

The door sprang open.

A boy stood before us. Or . . . a man? It was a little hard to tell. In both Fredtown and my parents' village, Rosi and I, as twelve-year-olds, had been the oldest kids. So I'd never seen a teenager in the flesh before. My Fred-parents *had* given me the most annoying lectures ever to prepare me for my body going through some pretty amazing changes over the next few years. I would become an adult in a transformation just as incredible as a caterpillar turning into a butterfly—though, disappointingly, without the cocoon stage, when I could have done nothing but sleep. (Was caterpillar-to-butterfly the analogy they used? Or was it the tadpole-into-a-frog thing? It wasn't like I really listened.)

Of course, the spin the Freds put on it was that it wasn't all fun and games and bulging muscles. They said adulthood required greater responsibility than childhood, blah, blah, blah, blah, blah.

They believed way too much in accepting responsibility. Taking on responsibility. Stepping up to responsibility. Volunteering for responsibility. Shouldering responsibility.

Responsibility—*blech*.

Anyhow, despite all those lectures, I'd never really been

able to imagine myself as an adult. Or even as an almost adult.

But this boy standing before me—Enu, I guessed—was clearly older than me, though maybe not yet full-grown.

He towered over me, and stood almost exactly eye to eye with Udans. His shoulders practically filled the doorway, every bit as wide as Udans's. Enu had somehow not bothered to put a shirt on—just an odd pair of shorts that hung down to his knees—and so I could see the ripple of muscles in his chest.

Oh man, I wanted to have muscles like that someday.

Forget looking like my dad. Was there any chance I would ever look like Enu?

He grinned, revealing a teasing dimple off to the side of his mouth that was a lot like mine. His eyes were a little darker than mine—more brownish-green than greenish-brown—and his hair was a little longer, standing up in thick, messy curls. But looking at Enu was like looking in some strange trick mirror: This *might* be what I would look like when I got a little older.

As much as I was studying Enu so carefully, he did not even bother looking at me.

"Udans!" he cried. "What'd you bring me? The usual?"

I took a step back. I imagined all the Freds in Fredtown hearing Enu and instantly fainting dead away. Enu hadn't even said hello—he'd gone straight to "What'd you bring me?"

Maybe a two-year-old could have gotten away with such rudeness back in Fredtown. Er, no, not even a kid that little. Back in Fredtown, pretty much as soon as kids could talk, they were expected to know not to ask for presents. They were expected to know to make visitors feel comfortable and welcome; they were expected to know to extend hospitality, not requests, to anyone showing up on their doorstep.

They were expected to know that life was about giving, not taking.

Even *I* knew that, and I probably hadn't listened to a Fred lecture all the way through since I was two.

To my surprise, Udans didn't scold Enu. Instead, he reached into his pants pocket and pulled out . . . was that a check? Some kind of money? Or just proof of a bank deposit?

Whatever it was, it looked official. I caught a glimpse of lots of zeros, in sets of three and separated by commas.

"Your portion for the week," Udans said, as he handed the paper to Enu.

"You know, you *could* do everything electronically," Enu said, pocketing it.

"It's good for you to be reminded of what your parents give you," Udans said sternly.

"Whatever." Enu shrugged and held out his hand again. "I can take care of Kiandra's, too."

"Oh no, you can't," a musical voice called from behind him. "Udans, don't trust him!"

A vision appeared in the doorway alongside Enu. I mean, it was a girl—a real girl—but it seemed like a vision, because the girl looked so much like a portrait that I'd seen back at my parents' house. My real parents, that is, not the Fred ones.

My parents' house was crazy fancy, and in their ridiculously formal dining room they had a practically life-size picture from their wedding day some twenty years ago: my dad, back when he actually had a thick head of hair, and my mom when her face was unlined and her hair was in ringlets crowned with daisies.

This girl—Kiandra?—wasn't wearing ringlets, daisies, or a wedding dress. She had on tiny shorts, just as fitted as Enu's were loose, and a T-shirt that said MINE, NOT YOURS. And she was younger than the girl in my parents' wedding portrait; it seemed possible that she was only a little older than me. But her face was so much like my mother's face that I almost felt a pang of homesickness. (Which was crazy—I'd known my mother for barely twenty-four hours, and she hadn't even said good-bye. Not to mention, I wasn't homesick for *any*one or *any*place. Not me.)

"So . . . ," Kiandra said. "Where's mine?"

Udans handed her a slip of paper like Enu's, and she leaned in to kiss him on the cheek.

"Okay, thanks, Udans," she said. She didn't glance my way either. I had never felt so invisible before. Or so young. "Now, we're kind of busy at the moment . . ."

She started to close the door.

What? They didn't invite Udans (or me) in? They didn't offer tea or coffee or lemonade or milk? They didn't ask Udans how he was, how his family was—or even how our parents were, back in their hometown?

Not even when Udans was giving them money—or a check or whatever—from their (our) father?

Udans held out his hand, holding the door open.

"That's not the only thing I brought you," he said, in a voice that held just a touch of sternness. He turned, and yanked me forward. Not that I'd been hiding behind Udans or anything.

Okay, maybe I was. Kind of.

"Meet your brother," Udans announced. "This is Edwy."

Kiandra and Enu both stared, as if they were noticing me for the first time. Then Kiandra started cracking up.

"Oh, Enu, it's like your mini-me! That's exactly how you looked three years ago!"

Enu glared at her.

And then *he* tried to shut the door. Right in my face.

CHAPTER TWELVE

I stuck my foot in the doorway.

"Are you kidding me?" I asked. "That's not fair!"

Back in Fredtown those words and that tone of mine would have struck fear in any kid around. The kids of Fredtown knew not to mess with me.

Enu *did* let the door bounce back open when it hit my foot. But he also joined his sister in laughing. And she started laughing harder, doubling over with giggles.

"I'd forgotten . . . Enu, that's how your voice used to sound!" she exclaimed. "So high and squeaky, like you'd been sucking helium. . . . Say something else, Little Enu!"

"My name is not Little Enu! I'm Edwy! And my voice is not high and squeaky!"

But for the first time ever, I noticed . . . maybe my voice was a little squeaky.

It certainly wasn't as deep as Enu's.

I clamped my mouth shut and glared. I *was* the best

glarer in Fredtown. Nobody could dispute that.

I mean, I used to be, back when I lived in Fredtown.

"Aww, I think you hurt his feelings," Enu said mockingly. He elbowed his sister. "Shut up, Kiandra!"

"Shut up, both of you," Udans said. He shoved past me and across the threshold, into the apartment. "Your parents would want you to invite us in, so we're not discussing any of this out in the hall."

Enu and Kiandra stepped aside to let Udans past. I trailed after him, and Enu swung the door shut behind us.

My jaw dropped when I saw the living room before us. It was huge—and hugely messy. Discarded clothes lay draped over the couch, the chairs, and the floor. A collection of apple cores seemed to be playing hide-and-go-seek in the potato-chip bags strewn across the end tables. A shallow cardboard box lay open on the coffee table in the middle of the room, with what looked like a fossilized slice of pepperoni pizza hanging halfway out. That pizza might have been there for *years*.

I could tell one thing. If I lived here with Enu and Kiandra, I would never have to pick up after myself.

Sweet.

Udans shoved aside a shirt that said GO, TEAM! in huge white letters and sat down on the low, dark-colored couch. I sat down beside him, but when Enu and Kiandra kept standing, I got back up.

"We have much to discuss," Udans said. "Everyone, *sit*."

Enu and Kiandra rolled their eyes—and, though I'd never admit this out loud to anyone, they were much better at eye rolling than I'd ever been. I practically wanted to take notes. But then both of them plopped down into the nearest chairs, sprawling sideways in a manner that seemed to say, *We're just sitting down because we want to—not because you told us to. And there's nothing you can say that will make us sit up straight and look respectful.*

"You too, Edwy," Udans said, grabbing my shoulders and pulling me down.

I would have fought against him, but . . . I didn't want Enu and Kiandra to see me lose. I tried to imitate their style, even muttering, "Now that I think of it, I am a little tired of standing."

Kiandra snickered, and I realized that even as I bent my knees, I'd accidentally kept my back ramrod straight and folded my hands in my lap like . . . well, like a good little Fred-trained child, raised to sit up straight and act respectful. I sprawled backward, but my neck touched something unpleasantly wet and mushy—was there *another* apple core hidden behind me on the couch? And had it maybe gone a little rotten?

I didn't let myself look. I pretended I didn't notice.

"Your father has decided that Edwy will live in your

extra bedroom," Udans informed Enu and Kiandra.

"What?" Enu protested. "We don't have an extra bedroom!"

Udans pointed silently at a half-open door.

"That's my video-game room!" Enu complained.

"Not anymore," Udans said. "You can move all your gaming equipment elsewhere. A bed and dresser will be arriving for Edwy in"—he looked at his watch—"about an hour."

Enu muttered something under his breath. Udans ignored him.

"Edwy has been enrolled in school," Udans continued. "The two of you will need to show him how to log on and sign up for classes."

"We're not babysitters," Kiandra said. "We're busy. We've got better things to do."

"What—your nails?" Udans asked, probably because Kiandra was looking down at her fingernails. For the first time, I noticed that they were painted purple and decorated with stars and swirls outlined in white.

"I resent that," Kiandra said, glaring at him. "It's not fair that you make it sound like a traditionally female interest might be inferior to whatever *you* want me to do. And that you make it sound like all I am capable of is beautifying my body, instead of—"

"Kiandra, are you trying to make this take a hundred

years?" Enu interrupted, punching her playfully on the shoulder. "When I've got a game to get back to?"

This was when any Fred would have sent them both to their rooms. I could just hear the gentle scolding: *You need to think about whether you are treating those around you with proper respect. You need to take a little time to ponder your words and actions more carefully. . . .*

Ugh, ugh, ugh. How many times had I heard that particular lecture back in Fredtown?

But it was weird. My stomach felt funny, and I thought maybe it was because Udans *wasn't* sending Enu and Kiandra to their rooms.

Maybe they were too old to be sent to their rooms. Could that happen? Even with kids who hadn't outgrown behaving like they *needed* to be sent to their rooms?

My stomach felt funnier than ever. I told myself it was just because of all that fizzy grape soda pop I'd drunk in Udans' truck.

"I don't need a babysitter anyway," I told Kiandra and Enu. "I can take care of myself!"

"So it's settled," Udans said, like he was pretending he hadn't seen or heard Kiandra and Enu do anything wrong. Or, um, me, either. The Freds wouldn't have liked my tone.

"I just need someone to tell me where the school is," I said, "and—"

Enu and Kiandra started laughing at me again.

"He thinks school is a *place*!" Kiandra moaned between giggles. "Don't you know anything?"

Was that a trick question? How could a school *not* be a place?

"Dude, you just log on to the computer, click the box that says, 'Homework completed for the day,' and that's it. You're done with school," Enu said.

I couldn't help myself. I turned to Udans. "But my dad said—" I began.

"Let me guess—did he lay it on thick, about what a prestigious boarding school you'd be attending?" Kiandra, still giggling, rolled her eyes even more dramatically than ever.

"Don't you tell him any different!" Enu shook a fist at me. Was that supposed to be a threat? "It's better for everyone if our parents *think* they're paying for intense, hard-core boarding school, but our grades are *really* coming from an easy-scam online school."

"It's not like they're ever going to be able to come here and check up on us," Kiandra said, shrugging. "Or like they'd believe you instead of us." She narrowed her eyes at me. "How much of a mini-Enu are you? Will you have trouble remembering to do the daily fake homework check?"

"I—"

She didn't seem to expect an answer. She didn't even listen.

"Even that is no big deal," she went on. "Let's say you forget for a whole week—even a whole grading period—and you're a little panicked about that. Well, then, a certain sister *is* capable of hacking into the site and making it *look* like you did all your homework—or at least did the one little minimal chore the school requires to *pretend* like you're doing homework . . ." Kiandra faked a cough and cleared her throat in an obnoxious way. "Not that anyone here might have needed that help." She muttered under her breath, "Stupid Enu. How much have you had to pay me?"

I glanced again at Udans, who just sat there, stony-faced.

Enu and Kiandra had to be joking, right? And was Udans in on the joke? I knew what school was. It was sitting in a classroom, and the teacher talking on and on and on—blah, blah, blah—about citizenship or life's purpose or something else boring. And then Rosi and I—it was always the two of us together, because we were the only twelve-year-olds in Fredtown—we'd have to do some project about the shape of fruit flies' eyes, or the rhyme scheme in poetry, or how democracy works. And Rosi would take the project seriously, and she'd worry because I just wanted to make the assignment sheet into a paper airplane and see if I could fly it into the teacher's hair. And Rosi—

I really couldn't think about Rosi right now.

Enu laughed louder.

"The kid actually looks worried," he chortled. "Like he thinks any of this matters!"

"It matters a lot to your parents," Udans said sternly. "It makes them so happy to think you are at a good school. 'Preparing the leaders of tomorrow'—isn't that what the website says? Your parents love getting the school's reports about how well you're doing."

"All the more reason to keep lying to them!" Enu crowed.

Udans dropped his head. Was he peering down at the crumbs in the carpet or . . . was he really, really sad?

None of this made any sense.

Kiandra sat up and put her hands on her hips.

"How do we know you're not just snowing us, Udans?" she asked. "How do we even know this boy is our brother? What if he's some relative of yours, or . . . or just someone whose family is bribing you to—"

"Would you like to talk to your parents about this matter?" Udans asked. "We can make a phone call right now."

Kiandra's eyes darted from side to side.

"No, that's okay," she said quickly. "I believe you."

What was *that* about? Why wouldn't Kiandra want to talk to our parents?

I could hear my Fred-parents' voices in my head, saying,

A child's love is the most important thing to any parent. Just spending time with you is what makes us happiest.

And the thing is, my Fred-parents drove me crazy. I thought they *were* crazy. And weird. And secretive. But they really seemed to mean it when they said that stupid little guilt-inducing line.

Didn't Kiandra want to make our real parents happy? Didn't she feel a teeny bit sad that she hadn't seen them in twelve years? Didn't she *want* to see them?

What *did* Kiandra and Enu want?

CHAPTER THIRTEEN

My bed and dresser arrived, and Udans directed the deliverymen to set it up in a room already overflowing with electronic gear. Enu kept darting in and out, carrying boxes and cords and odd-shaped items he called game controllers. The whole time he complained: "Oh man, I'm going to have to move *this* gaming system too? Did you have to order such a big bed? How much room does a little kid actually need?"

"I'm not a little kid," I told him, but he acted like he hadn't even heard me.

And then everything was arranged, and the deliverymen left. And then Udans walked toward the front door.

"Wait!" I called after him.

He turned around, his pirate ponytail whipping to the side.

"Why?" he asked.

Because I don't think Kiandra and Enu want me here. Because I don't know how they'll treat me once you're gone.

Because I don't know enough about Refuge City yet. Because I'm worried about my friend Rosi, and maybe if you stay, I'll work up the courage to ask you to check on her or . . .

I couldn't say any of that.

"Don't I get money like you gave Kiandra and Enu?" I asked. My Fred-parents would have been horrified. I enjoyed imagining their distressed expressions.

"Oh, I almost forgot," Udans said. He reached into his pocket and pulled out a thin plastic card. He held it out to me.

"That's not what you gave them!" I complained.

"I haven't set up your account yet," he said. "You can use this debit card until then. But . . . the old man can see what you pay for."

"You mean, my parents trust them more than me?" I asked indignantly.

Udans leaned close, like he was going to share a secret.

"Or he doesn't want them to know he's giving you more," he whispered in my ear. "Because you need all those new clothes, remember?"

"Oh yeah."

He winked at me.

"I'll be back in a couple days," he added. "Or maybe next week. As soon as I can."

And then he walked out the door. And I was alone.

I'd been alone before. Of course I had. Until the night before, I'd thought I was an only child. Back in Fredtown I'd spent a million hours privately dreaming up pranks and schemes to drive the Freds crazy. Back in my parents' hometown, I'd gone fishing by myself; I'd walked all over the place by myself.

Still, in Fredtown I'd always had little kids looking up to me, asking me constantly, *What are you doing? Can I help? Can I play with you?* I'd always had someone to hang out with, if I wanted to. And when we were traveling to my parents' hometown—away from all the Freds, forever—Rosi and I had promised to watch out for each other. Every time I was alone after that, I'd been thinking about telling Rosi what I saw. I'd been planning to ask her questions, to see if she'd figured out any more than I had.

But Rosi wasn't here in Refuge City with me. I tried not to think about the exact promise we'd made to each other on the plane from Fredtown. She knew I wasn't good at keeping promises. And this time it really wasn't my fault. But if Udans was right about everything, I might never see her again. All I had now was Kiandra and Enu.

Maybe they're not so bad, I told myself. *Maybe . . . maybe they were just acting up to get rid of Udans. I'd do that. Maybe it's going to be great having a brother and a sister!*

I went into "my" room, where Enu was sprawled on the

floor in front of the one remaining TV he'd insisted on keeping in place there, after the deliverymen moved three others to the living room. He had earbuds in his ears and held one of the "game controllers" in his hands. He kept waving it around and jabbing at buttons on top of it. On the TV screen it looked like spaceships were exploding and . . . were those dead bodies falling out? Dead astronauts?

I had to be wrong about that. Nobody would make a game involving dead bodies.

"Can I play too?" I asked Enu.

He didn't answer. He must not have heard me. I tugged on the wire of the left earbud, and it came out of his ear, falling into my hand.

"Give me that!" Enu growled, grabbing the earbud and stuffing it back into his ear. On the TV screen a spaceship sped by, dignified and majestic. It didn't explode. No dead bodies fell out.

"See what you made me do?" Enu complained. He stabbed a finger against the controller, and the word PAUSED appeared on the screen. "I had a perfect score until *you* came in! Even on an old, easy game like this, you mess me up! Go away and leave me alone!"

"But . . . this is *my* room," I said.

Enu grabbed the front of my shirt and pulled me close. He curled his lip and stared me straight in the eye.

"It's only *your* room when *I* say you can use it!" he said. "Now—get out of here. Quit bugging me!"

He shoved me away. I managed to avoid hitting my head on the wall only because I have good reflexes.

I stayed crouched exactly where I fell for a moment before I decided to say, "You know what? I think I'll go hang out with Kiandra. What you're doing looks boring."

I got up slowly—like it'd been my decision to huddle down against the wall in the first place. I noticed that Enu had gone back to staring at the screen. I walked back into the living room. Kiandra was sitting upside down on one of the couches, her legs against the back of the couch, her feet against the wall, her head leaned backward on the part of the couch where she was supposed to bend her knees. I wished I'd thought to try out that pose in Fredtown, because it would have made my Fred-parents' eyes bulge out and their voices strain to stay a normal pitch and volume even as they scolded something like, *Young man, do you know what happens when we don't take care of our possessions properly? What do you think will happen if you're constantly leaving footprints on the wall? Whose job do you think it should be to wash them off?*

It was more fun to imagine their distress than it had ever been to listen to their lectures.

I walked over to the couch and lay down in the same position as Kiandra. I had to stretch my legs a little farther to be able to touch the wall with my feet. I leaned my head back—upside down, like hers. She had a laptop computer cradled in her lap—also upside down—and I craned my neck so I could look at the screen.

"What are you doing?" I asked.

She tilted the laptop away so I couldn't see.

"Nothing I want to share with you," she muttered.

I couldn't help it: I looked around automatically, expecting some Fred to materialize out of nowhere to tell Kiandra she was being rude, and that was unacceptable. The Freds totally believed in sharing. Why wasn't she considering my feelings? Didn't she care?

But it wasn't like I *wanted* any Freds around to tell her that. No. Of course not.

I reached out and yanked the laptop back toward me. On the screen I caught a quick glimpse of the words *Refuge City Scholars Academy Computer Science Homework, Week of—* I started laughing.

"You're doing homework, and *that's* what you're afraid to let me see?" I mocked. "What—are you a really bad student, and you're ashamed that I'll find out you're doing, like, second-grade work, and still failing at it?"

She wanted to go rude? She should know she was messing with the Fredtown Champion of Rudeness.

Kiandra hit something on the keyboard that made the

whole screen go blank. She snapped the laptop shut; I had to snatch my hand back or she would have smashed my fingers.

"For your information, I am a very *good* student," she said. She glanced toward the room where Enu was playing video games, and lowered her voice. "I just don't want anyone to know I actually do the homework."

Okay, that was weird. What was this, backward world? In Fredtown it had been *not* doing homework that kids had to hide. Kids like me.

Kiandra gave my shoulder a shove.

"Everyone I know with little brothers says it's awful," she muttered. "*So* annoying."

Whoa. Who knew I was capable of being an Annoying Younger Brother? Just by using the same skills that made me a Bad Influence on Younger Kids back in Fredtown?

But a quick memory flashed across my mind of Rosi with her little brother, Bobo, walking down the aisle of the plane that was going to take us back to our parents' hometown. Rosi had had her hand on Bobo's shoulder, protecting him. Keeping him safe from *me*.

She always took care of her little brother. She never shoved him or told him he was annoying.

So what? I told myself. *Bobo's, like, five. I'm twelve. I don't need a big brother or big sister—or anyone!—taking care of me. Who cares if Kiandra and Enu don't treat me like kids treated their little brothers in Fredtown? This isn't Fredtown!*

But my mouth opened and words started coming out before I had time to think. That happened to me a lot. Just . . . not usually with these particular words.

"What do you think our parents would do if they knew you were being mean to me?" I asked.

Kiandra shrugged.

"What can they do?" she taunted. "They're not here! They can't do anything!"

Was that true? I thought about arguing that they might stop giving her money. Or they might tell Udans to give her a time-out the next time he came to Refuge City. Or . . .

Or they might take Kiandra's side over mine. They've been sending her money and taking care of her for years. They didn't even meet me until the day before yesterday.

"If . . . ," I began helplessly.

"Oh, I get it," Kiandra mocked. "Do you really think they have any control over us from back in Cursed Town?"

I made myself laugh at what Kiandra had said.

"'Cursed Town'?" I mocked. "Do our parents know you call their home Cursed Town? What if I tattle and get you in trouble for that?"

Kiandra flashed me a puzzled look.

"Kid, everyone calls Cursed Town 'Cursed Town.' That's its name."

"Oh, right," I scoffed. "You think I'm going to fall for that? Like someone hundreds of years ago started a village and said, 'Hey, I know what will make this a successful place. I'm going to give it a name that makes everyone think there's a curse on it!' You must think I'm really dumb! Everyone knows the real name of our parents' hometown is . . ."

It suddenly occurred to me that I had never *heard* the name of our parents' hometown. Not once. Even the Freds had never spoken it. They just called it "your real home." Nobody in my nearly two days of living in that town had mentioned it. And I'd walked all over the town—there hadn't been any signs saying what the town's name was.

But if your home's name included the word "cursed," would you want to advertise that?

I thought of the horrid, burned-out place in my parents' hometown that I'd showed Rosi the night Udans "kidnapped" me.

It had seemed like a cursed place.

Kiandra opened her laptop again.

"Proof," she muttered. "Here's a map."

She tilted the screen toward me. I'd only ever used a computer for schoolwork—the Freds had this idea that it might be bad for kids to spend too much time staring at a screen. But I knew enough about computers to be able to tell that Kiandra had called up an official-looking map site. She zoomed in to show me Refuge City and all the area around it. I could pick out the mountain range that stood at the outer edge of Refuge City, and the winding road that Udans had used, bringing me here. I followed that road back out into the flat-looking countryside. Back, back, back . . . not long after the road crossed a thick, forbidding-looking black line, it did indeed lead to a dot labeled CURSED TOWN.

Kiandra pointed the tip of her purple fingernail at that label. "See?"

"You could have hacked into that site and just made it say that," I accused, still doubtful. "That makes more sense than someone naming a place Cursed Town on purpose."

"That wasn't the *original* name of the town," Kiandra admitted. "But the name changed after . . . you know. The war."

I remembered what my father had told me about the war in his hometown. I tried not to let Kiandra see me shiver.

"Oh yeah?" I challenged. "Well, if this map's for real, what's that?"

I pointed at the thick black line that separated the territory between Refuge City and Cursed Town.

"The border," Kiandra said, and even she sounded serious and scared. "The line that almost no one is allowed to cross. The line that Udans just smuggled you past. Our father must have spent a fortune bribing everyone to make that happen." She hit my shoulder again, this time with her hand balled up into a fist. "A fortune that *should* have been part of Enu's and my inheritance."

"Well, excuse me," I muttered. "*I* didn't ask to be smuggled here. I didn't ask anyone to spend money on me."

Kiandra's eyes widened. I could see the flecks of green in her dark iris.

"You really are dumb, then," she said. "You should have asked. You should have *begged*. You should have known the minute you arrived in Cursed Town that it's a despicable place. And . . . dangerous."

Rosi, I thought. *Rosi's still there.*

Was *Rosi* in danger?

CHAPTER FOURTEEN

"You any good at basketball, pipsqueak?" Enu asked, emerging from my room.

I did an amazing somersault: One minute I was hanging backward and upside down on the couch; the next I was landing on my feet and facing Enu. I looked down at Kiandra to see if she was impressed. I shouldn't have—she still had a solemn expression on her face from talking about Cursed Town and danger.

She was probably just teasing, I told myself. *Telling spooky stories just to scare me. So she could laugh at me.*

I'd, um, done that a time or two to little kids back in Fredtown. But not the ones who would cry. Just the ones who could take a joke.

Does Kiandra think I can take a joke? Does this means she likes me?

I wasn't used to worrying about things like that. It was so weird being the youngest kid, not one of the oldest.

"Am I any good at basketball?" I repeated Enu's question. "I was the best twelve-year-old boy in all of Fredtown!"

That wasn't technically a lie. Not at all. Enu didn't have to know that I'd been the *only* twelve-year-old boy in all of Fredtown. Which made me both the best *and* the worst of the twelve-year-old male basketball players.

I could have just said "best twelve-year-old," except . . . well, Rosi was actually better at basketball than I was. In the past year she'd grown taller than me, and that made her a lot better at rebounds.

My Fred-parents said sometimes girls got their growth before boys. They predicted that I would almost certainly be taller than Rosi when we were both adults.

Not that I'd ever said I was worried about my height back in Fredtown.

Or about Rosi now . . .

Enu didn't have to know any of that.

He paused in the kitchen and downed half a carton of orange juice in what seemed to be a single gulp.

"If you promise not to talk about that Fredtown, you can come play with my guys," he said. "We're down a player because of Wong Li's broken ankle."

"That's what happens when people jump off cars," Kiandra muttered.

I wanted to ask, *Did one of your friends really jump off a car? From the roof or just the hood? Or the bumper? Was the car moving when he jumped?*

I wanted to ask, *Why can't I talk about Fredtown? Why did Udans warn me about that too?*

But I also wanted to go play basketball with Enu and his friends, and I was afraid he wouldn't let me if I asked too many questions.

"And don't say you're twelve," Enu said. "If anyone asks, say you're a stunted thirteen-year-old."

Why? Because . . . then there's no way I would have come from Fredtown? I thought.

Rosi and I were the oldest kids who'd been taken to Fredtown. The Freds started taking babies there the very day we were both born. (And yes, it was really annoying that she and I shared the same birthday.)

But why did Enu care?

"No one's going to believe that kid's thirteen," Kiandra scoffed. "Not with that squeaky voice."

"Obviously he got the leftover genes in the family," Enu said. "The subpar ones. After I took all the good ones. Because I was born first, I got the best."

"Genes don't work that way!" Kiandra protested, even as I complained, "That's not fair!"

Enu dumped the last half of the orange juice carton down his throat.

"Deal or no deal?" he asked.

"Are you playing at the AZ?" I asked.

I wanted Enu or Kiandra to marvel, *Wow! He knows people call the Athletic Zone the AZ! It's like he's lived in Refuge City his whole life!*

But Enu just grunted.

"Where else?" he asked.

Twenty minutes later—after waiting for a delivery from an athletics store of all the "gear" Enu said I needed—I changed into net-fabric shorts and a light T-shirt and brand-new basketball shoes, tugged a backpack over my shoulder, and followed Enu out the door. We took the elevator down to the street, and I braced myself for a repeat of the challenges of walking behind Udans.

But Enu took up half the sidewalk; the crowd parted before him. He strutted, and people got out of the way.

It was really easy to walk in his wake.

I couldn't resist asking why.

"How do you do that?" I asked.

"Do what?" he muttered.

"Get people to clear a path for you," I said. "Get them to move away as you're coming toward them."

"Do they?" he asked, as if he hadn't noticed.

"Um, yeah," I said. A woman teetering on crazy-tall shoes and a man wearing a business suit moved to the side in front of us. "Nobody did that for Udans."

Enu snorted.

"Udans is a country chicken," he said. "His clothes shout *bumpkin*. And he walks around like he's afraid someone might notice him and send him home. Watch."

Enu hunched over his shoulders and kept his gaze low, peering back and forth.

The crowd started pressing in on us.

Enu threw his shoulders back again, lifted his head— and glared straight at a man who was about to brush against Enu's shoulder.

The man instantly veered to the right, out of Enu's way.

"Udans looks like a pirate," I said, feeling a weird sense of loyalty.

"A pirate?" Enu scoffed. "Maybe one who's not any good at finding treasure. One who's scared to do anything but follow the captain's orders."

"Our father's the captain, you mean," I said, stretching out my legs trying to keep up with Enu. He really was a lot taller than me.

Enu rolled his eyes.

"Duh," he said. "Our father's a crime lord. He's cool."

Did "cool" mean something in Refuge City that it didn't mean back in Fredtown or, uh, Cursed Town? Was having a father who was a crime lord something to be proud of?

What was a crime lord, anyway? Just a thief?

"Down here," Enu said, pointing me toward a set of stairs that descended beneath the sidewalk. "We're taking the subway."

At the bottom of the stairs we passed into a gleaming white passageway. Doors opened, and Enu tugged me into a train car. The seats sparkled, and I started to sit down.

"Don't bother," Enu said. "We're only going one stop."

The doors shut and opened again a moment later; we were someplace new.

I stepped out into a passageway painted bright orange, right on Enu's heels.

"How does that work?" I whispered in amazement. "I didn't even feel the train move!"

"Who knows? Who cares?" Enu said with a shrug. "It works. That's all that matters."

That wasn't at all how Freds would have seen things. If any Fred had been with us, they would have said, *That is a great question. Let's think about this. Do you think it's hydraulics? Pulleys? Magnetics? Make your guess, and then we'll do some research and test your hypothesis. . . .*

I never wanted to agree with the Fred way of doing anything but . . . I did want to know how the train worked.

Maybe I could research it on my own. Later.

Enu led me out onto the street. One of the towering

domes I'd seen from Udans's truck hovered directly in front of us. Enu started bounding up the stairs toward the dome; then he stopped and turned around.

"One other thing you shouldn't talk about," he said, bending toward me and talking softly, even though no one else was around us. "Don't say anything about the fact that all my friends are different colors."

"Different colors?" I repeated blankly. "Isn't everyone different colors? I mean, my eyes are green and my hair is brown and my lips are kind of browny-red and—"

Enu punched my arm. I was starting to think that that was Enu's favorite way to communicate. Kiandra's, too.

"Don't be a smart aleck," he said. "I mean they all have different-colored skin. Wong Li and Alphonse Xu are mostly Asian, and Hector Goodleaf must be, like, almost pure African, and I think Jorge Colon's family came from somewhere in South America, and—"

"You really think I'd say something about what color skin people have?" I asked indignantly. "Who would do that? Who would care?"

Enu met my gaze with narrowed eyes.

"Someone from Cursed Town would do that," he muttered.

"I'm not from Cursed Town!" I protested. "I was there for barely twenty-four hours!"

Enu jerked his head back and forth, looking around as if he was afraid someone might have heard us.

"Chill, dude," he said. "You've got to admit, I don't really know anything about you. You could be anyone."

"I'm your *brother*," I said, and it was embarrassing, how much it sounded like I was begging him to agree. "We're here in Refuge City *together*. We're *family*."

"It's *Ref* City," Enu corrected me. "Nobody calls it Refuge City except country bumpkins like Udans. And our parents. And . . . try to act like you've always lived here. Don't say anything about where you did or didn't come from."

So I wasn't supposed to say anything about Fredtown or Cursed Town.

What was I allowed to say?

CHAPTER FIFTEEN

Enu's friends were all giants. Considering that I'd only ever played basketball with little kids, Freds, and Rosi, it turned out that I might as well never have played basketball before in my life. From the first tipoff I could tell: In this game here at the AZ, I might as well have been playing with giant sequoia trees that could run. I might as well have been a little bug crawling around on the ground squeaking, *Please. Don't anybody step on me.*

But I *did* know all the rules of basketball—oh, how the Freds liked us knowing rules. So when the monstrous creature I was supposed to be guarding caught the ball, dribbled once, then took three quick steps without dribbling again, I squeaked out (from my position halfway back the court from him), "Hey! That's traveling! You have to forfeit the ball!"

"Nobody cares," the gigantic kid said lazily, even as he sank the ball into the basket.

He was so much taller than me, it felt like he could have

stepped on me and flattened me completely. I waited for the rest of his team—which included Enu—to turn on him and scold him for bad sportsmanship. That's what would have happened in Fredtown. Then there would be apologies, and I would be expected to pretend to forgive the kid, and . . .

The other team didn't scold him. They cheered.

"Didn't you hear me?" I protested. "Didn't anyone else *see*? He just cheated!"

"Dude, shut up," Enu hissed at me, running up beside me. His face was red. "You're embarrassing me. Everybody cheats."

"Not—" I began, then clamped my mouth shut. Because I'd been about to say, *Not in Fredtown. Not my friend Rosi. Not ever.*

"Keep playing," Enu yelled at all his friends.

He gave me a little swat on the rear.

"Be cool," he whispered. "Or I'll send you home. I will."

Did he mean *home to the apartment we share with Kiandra*? Or did he maybe even mean *home to Cursed Town? Home to Fredtown?*

I'm never going back to Fredtown or Cursed Town, I told myself. *Refuge City—I mean, Ref City—this is where I belong.*

The ball zipped past me, over my head—zooming from the fingertips of one giant sequoia tree to another—and I jumped for it. I might as well have been jumping for a rocket ship in orbit around the Earth. But at least I was trying.

After that I ran up and down the court, doing my best to keep up. But it was like my complaining about the cheating had made me invisible. Nobody on my team passed to me. The opposing team didn't bother sidestepping me. They just knocked me down when I was in the way. And nobody gave me a hand back up. They didn't even glance at me.

This was *not* how I was used to being treated. Back in Fredtown I'd been Edwy the Amazing, Edwy the Bad Influence, Edwy Whom All the Younger Kids Wanted to Imitate. Even when I got in trouble, I had all these kids watching me, their eyes wide and awed, as if they were all thinking, *Edwy's so much braver than me! Someday I want to be like him! I want to break the rules too!*

Was there any punishment that was worse than being ignored?

"Water break!" someone called, and everyone went to the sidelines to gulp down whole liters of liquid in a single swallow. I'd just managed to extract my own water bottle from my backpack when a whistle went off and everybody else was back on the court.

Nobody waited for me. Not even Enu. Even he didn't call out, *Wait! Edwy's not ready yet!*

I took a sip of water, but it tasted tinny and disgusting

in my mouth. I was panting too hard to swallow.

What if I threw up?

How much would *that* embarrass Enu?

Suddenly I wanted to embarrass him. I wanted to embarrass everyone. At the very least I wanted to force everyone to look at me.

One of the opposing sequoia monsters came dribbling down the court, just the other side of the line from me. I stepped across the line and buried my head in his stomach, knocking him off course, practically knocking him to the wooden floor. The ball bounced wildly, and I snagged it from his grasp. I held the ball the way a little kid might—with both arms wrapped around it, not bouncing it at all. I took off running toward my team's basket, and as soon as I was close, I flung the ball into the air.

The ball teetered on the rim and then slipped in.

"Three points!" I screamed, holding my arms in the air. Even here this had to be the sign of victory.

I'd shot from much too close to get more than two points for that basket. I'd traveled. I'd fouled the opposing team's player. I'd practically tackled him, and I could hear a Fred voice in my head scolding, *Now, what do you think would happen if everyone tried to play that way? Wouldn't you get mad if your opponents did that? Think how you'd feel if you had a breakaway that someone else ruined, not even playing fair?*

But the sequoia trees around me laughed. My own team gathered around me and high-fived me. They slapped me on the back.

"Way to show *him*!" someone called.

"This kid's got heart!" someone else marveled.

"How'd you sink that basket?" someone asked.

I puffed out my chest: *Oh yeah! Go, me! I'm so bad I'm good!*

But that Fred voice kept talking in my head. No—maybe it was Rosi's voice.

People are cheering for you because you cheated? And that makes you happy?

What's wrong with you?

CHAPTER SIXTEEN

Enu taught me how to play video games. I destroyed lots and lots of virtual spaceships. I killed lots and lots of virtual astronauts. I even learned how to cheat at those video games.

Kiandra showed me how to sign up for classes and fake doing my homework.

That was a kind of cheating too.

I learned how to order any type of food I wanted, anytime I wanted it: pizza at midnight, fried rice at three a.m., banana splits for breakfast.

This felt like cheating at food.

I went back to play basketball again and again with Enu's friends—Wong Li's broken ankle was taking a long time to heal. Now they said I was a "scrappy" player; my teammates said I was so good because I could run between the opposing team's knees.

And because I could cheat really well.

Enu's friends kind of became my friends. At least, they

rubbed my sweaty head at the end of every game and muttered, "See you next time."

They wouldn't have done that if they didn't like me, right?

I knew they weren't like Freds, pretending to like everyone.

Sometimes, when the basketball games ended after dark, Enu and I would walk home through the well-dressed crowds, and the lights of the city would already be cranked up to their greatest intensity. The enormous TV screens in the public squares hovered high above our heads, showing the actions of people who looked as tall as skyscrapers. The streets stayed as bright as day, even without the sun; it was like all of Ref City was one big glow. Sometimes the blinding lights and the noise of Ref City made my eyes blur and my ears ring. Sometimes then I'd hear the whisper in my head that I still thought of as Rosi's voice: *Edwy, what are you doing? What about that huge, dead, burned place we saw in our parents' hometown? What do you think it means? Are you even trying to find out? And don't you remember how we promised to watch out for each other?*

When that happened, I'd turn to Enu and say as loudly as I could—because I had to talk over the noise of Ref City *and* the voice in my head—"Hey, want to stop for barbecued ribs? Or would you rather get ice cream?"

Then one day, long after I'd stopped expecting him, Udans came back.

Enu, Kiandra, and I were still sleeping when he knocked at the door. So what if it was two o'clock in the afternoon? We'd been up most of the night.

"I know the three of you are in there!" he called through the locked door. "Your bioscan sensors show exactly where you are!"

Bioscan sensors? Huh?

I stumbled to the door and opened it.

Just a week and a half in Ref City made me see Udans differently. His clothes *were* ragged and countrified. His scars didn't look tough and adventurous anymore, just ugly. He didn't hold himself proudly enough.

He really needs to get himself some swagger, I thought.

"Your parents want to talk to you," he said.

I gasped.

"They're here? They came with you this time?" I asked.

I heard a snort behind me.

"He means by videoconference call," Kiandra muttered, stumbling sleepily out of her bedroom. "So, Udans, are you sure the lines of communication with Cursed Town are actually open right now?"

"The word is that authorities believe it will help morale," Udans said.

"Theirs, maybe," Kiandra said under her breath. "Not ours."

"Think about what your parents have sacrificed for you—" Udans began.

"Yeah, yeah," Kiandra said with a scornful eye roll. "You've got to give us time to get ready." Her gaze fell on me. "You. Clean all the pizza boxes and food wrappers off the couch."

"You're not the boss of me," I said, which was this great expression I'd learned from Enu only the day before. I wished I'd known to say that back in Fredtown.

"Today I am," Kiandra told me. "And . . . when you ordered clothes last week, did you get any suits?"

I must have looked at her blankly, because she added, "Jacket, tie, button-down shirt . . ."

"Of course not!" I said.

I'd ordered athletic pants and shorts, T-shirts, and—in case it ever got cold—sweatshirts.

She picked up a nearby laptop.

"Then I'm ordering a suit for you now," she muttered. "What are you—size twelve? Oh, whatever. We'll use masking tape to make the sleeves look shorter, if we have to."

Kiandra was a little scary like this. I actually picked up a pizza box from the couch and started carrying it toward the trash.

"Work faster!" she cried, even as she typed on the laptop with one hand and hit Enu's door with the other. "Ten-minute warning to parental conference call!" she called in through his door.

It was actually fifteen minutes later by the time the three of us sat down stiffly on the couch—now clear of all debris. The suit Kiandra had ordered for me had just arrived, and I was still stuffing my arms through the sleeves when Kiandra balanced her laptop on the coffee table and typed in some sort of code.

"Three, two, one . . . ," Kiandra muttered.

And then her face lit up with the most radiant smile I'd ever seen.

"Hello, dear father and mother," she cooed.

"Greetings," Enu rumbled in his deepest voice.

"Uh, hi?" I mumbled.

I felt a hand at my back—Kiandra tugging down the hem of my coat so it didn't bunch up. I could see the three of us reflected in the computer screen: Nobody would have known that we'd all been sound asleep just twenty minutes earlier. Kiandra had put on a sky-blue lace dress and wrapped a demure pink ribbon around her hair; Enu sat tall in a dark suit and deep purple shirt. He'd even slicked down his hair.

My hair was slicked down too, which made me appear older. My suit was gray, but it was just as formal as my brother's. I did kind of look like a miniature Enu. Or he looked like an overgrown version of me.

Kiandra reached out and angled the laptop screen differently. The reflection vanished, and I could see my parents sitting in their living room together.

Our mother seemed to have tears in her eyes.

"All our children, all together," she murmured. "All safe. I just had to be sure. . . ."

"Of course we're safe here in Refuge City," Kiandra said soothingly. "And we're all progressing so well in our studies. . . ."

"Udans said you wished to speak with us?" Enu asked, making it sound as if he were eager to hear from our parents, as if he hadn't awakened cursing them and complaining, *Why would they want to speak to us now? What if we don't want to talk to them?*

"It is enough just to see your shining faces, just to know you are safe and happy," our mother whispered. But her eyes darted to the side.

My father's rocklike face stayed hard.

"Yesterday I learned how to bake a cherry pie," Kiandra said, her tone breezy and casual now.

I started to say, *Huh? When? Where? What did you do with that pie?* Because as far as I'd been able to tell, she'd spent the entire day—and night—hunched over her laptop. That's how she spent most of her time.

Enu dug his elbow into my side in a way that wouldn't

show up on the webcam, because we were sitting too close together.

"And that pie was delicious, wasn't it, Edwy?" Enu asked. "Our sister's great at baking!"

Kiandra was usually so busy on her computer that I rarely even saw her eat. She was more likely to nibble on leftover pizza crusts from what Enu and I ordered.

"We're so proud of you," our mother murmured. Her eyes glistened.

"And Edwy and I love our business courses," Enu said. "Maybe we can open a Refuge City subsidiary of your business in a few years."

A muscle twitched in our father's cheek.

"No need to worry about any of that yet," he said. But even I could hear the pride in his voice.

Enu and Kiandra are shameless, I thought. *Shameless liars. What would they do if our parents showed up here expecting a home-cooked meal? Or . . . expecting to talk business with sons who haven't paid attention to any class, to any schoolwork at all?*

Udans hovered just on the other side of Kiandra's laptop. He nodded encouragingly at Enu, Kiandra, and me. He gave us a double thumbs-up.

"And how are the two of you doing?" Kiandra asked our parents. "Is your health good?"

She sounded every bit as solicitous as the most Fred-like adult in Fredtown. She sounded like she actually *cared*. But this was Kiandra. Kiandra who communicated by punching my arm almost as often as Enu did. Kiandra who wouldn't normally have been caught dead wearing a ribbon in her hair. Kiandra who made fun of my parents constantly

"Oh yes, yes," our mother nodded blithely. "We are both fine."

What if our mother and father were lying every bit as much as Kiandra and Enu were lying? What if they were sitting there nodding and smiling while their lives were in danger?

I remembered what Kiandra had said about Cursed Town being a dangerous place.

I remembered that I didn't even know if Rosi was in danger.

Would my parents know? Would they tell me? Would they tell me the *truth*?

It was funny. Back in Fredtown, where lying wasn't allowed, I was a great liar. I *loved* lying. But now I could practically feel myself breaking out in hives from all the lies around me. It was like I'd suddenly become allergic.

And it wasn't just because the suit Kiandra had ordered for me was itchy.

"Everyone is thriving here," my father said, beaming from the computer at his three children.

That did it. I remembered the burned-out, dead part of my parents' hometown that Rosi and I had explored together.

I remembered the rows of falling-down houses where most of the residents of Cursed Town lived. I was no expert on what houses should look like, but even I could tell that the people in those houses hadn't been thriving. Some of them maybe weren't even surviving.

I remembered that my parents' hometown seemed so thoroughly cursed that that had become part of its name.

Before Kiandra and Enu could stop me, I jumped to my feet.

"Stop lying!" I demanded. "What's the truth? Tell us!"

CHAPTER SEVENTEEN

Enu and Kiandra yanked me back into my seat on the couch, but not before I'd managed to scream out, "What caused the war in Cursed Town? Why—"

Enu clapped his hand over my mouth.

"Edwy is . . . working on a project for school," Kiandra said faintly. "And, you know. He wants to make sure all his facts are . . . accurate."

I squirmed against Enu's grasp, but he was much, much stronger than me.

"Your school requires a project about . . . about our town?" our mother moaned.

I bit Enu's hand, and that made him pull it away for a moment.

"I just want to know the truth!" I cried. "What really happened?"

On the computer screen my father sat up straight.

"That's my boy," he said, as if I'd done something to be proud of. "Would that school of yours tell you what really happened to us? Would they tell the story the right way? You are all old enough to know."

Just past the laptop I'd seen Udans start to lunge for me, but now he pulled back. He started grimly shaking his head. On the computer screen our mother was doing the same thing.

"We *are* old enough to know the truth," I agreed with my father. "We're old enough to know everything."

Beside me Enu seemed to be imitating our father's technique of making his face as hard and emotionless as stone. I glanced toward Kiandra to see if she was doing the same thing, but she was reaching for a pad of paper nestled in the food wrappers of the end table. (It was off camera, so none of us had bothered to clean up that mess.)

"I'll take notes," Kiandra said. "That way Edwy can just listen."

On the screen our father leaned forward.

"You have to go back several generations to understand," he said.

"Yes, yes, of course," Kiandra murmured.

I glanced at the notepad braced against her lace-covered knees. She was just doodling now, drawing a row of frowning faces with Xs for eyes.

"Once there was a tribe of men too mighty to stay in one place," our father intoned in a solemn voice. "Those were our ancestors."

Kiandra seemed to be writing more than our father had said. I glanced down; she'd scrawled, *It was a tribe of men* and *women. The women were important too.*

She was still writing: *. . . and, really, they were probably just too poor to own any land. So that's why they became nomads.*

"Our people wandered the Earth, learning new customs and skills everywhere they went," our father continued.

Stealing, pillaging, slinking away in the dark of night . . . appeared on Kiandra's notepad.

"And our people were admired for their fierceness and beauty everywhere they went," our father said. "But they were like chameleons. Their appearance as a people changed, depending on where they went. When they went to the north, their skin became lighter and their hair straighter. When they went to the south, their skin got darker and their hair curlier."

He's making it sound all mysterious, but that's what happens when people intermarry with other tribes with different traits. It's genetics, not magic.

"But always, our people were known for their striking green eyes," our father said.

Now, that was probably a genetic modification. Green eyes wouldn't normally have been dominant, Kiandra wrote. *But he's going to act like everyone in our tribe had them, no matter what.*

"It was amazing," our father continued. "Every child of our tribe had those stunning green eyes."

See? Kiandra wrote. *They probably gave away any child without green eyes.*

I automatically touched my face, as if I needed to point to my own eyes. I'd never really thought about it—who cared about eye color?—but my eyes were greener than Enu's or Kiandra's.

Does that mean my parents think I'm more valuable? I wondered. *Because I'm more like our amazing ancestors?*

Any Fred would have been horrified that I was thinking that way. In Fredtown they'd said again and again (and again and again and again, until I wanted to puke) that it didn't matter what anyone looked like. What was important about any human beings was what they thought, how they acted, what they did, how they treated other people. Things that weren't just skin-deep.

But I'd lived a day and a half in Cursed Town. I'd lived a week and a half in Ref City.

I knew now: Outside Fredtown not everyone thought like a Fred.

"After many a generation, after traveling for centuries and absorbing the wisdom and skills of the rest of the world, our ancestors decided to return to their homeland," our father went on.

Probably they were kicked out of every other land, Kiandra wrote. *Because of the pillaging and stealing wives. Bad ancestors!*

My stomach twisted. What was wrong with Kiandra, that she had to make our father's story into something awful? Maybe our ancestors had been noble and wise. Maybe they'd even been magical, with their extraordinary green eyes.

"When our ancestors got back to their homeland," our father said, "they found that outsiders had invaded and taken over."

Kiandra wrote something on her notepad, but I didn't look at it this time.

"Our ancestors nobly tried to share everything they had learned in their travels," our father said. "They tried to show the interlopers better ways to grow crops, better ways to build houses, better ways to raise their children."

"But the intruders, they were stupid and cruel," our mother said, adding to the story for the very first time. "They, they . . ."

"They killed our people," our father said. "Just because they were different. They killed my parents and grandparents. And my brothers and sisters."

I jerked back. It was that word, "killed." Could people really kill other people? Was that what happened in a war?

And how had my father skipped from talking about ancestors and ancient tribes to the death of his parents and grandparents and siblings? To *his* generation, just one generation before mine?

I couldn't look at Kiandra's notepad. I couldn't look at

Kiandra or Enu. I couldn't even look at my mother and father, on the computer screen right in front of me.

"O-kay, then," Enu said. "You answered Edwy's question. Thanks. I'm sure that's all he really needed to know. I bet you two have lots of things to do today—we'll be so happy to talk to you the next time. . . ."

Enu squeezed my arm, as if that could stop me from asking any other questions. He needn't have bothered. I couldn't speak. If I'd opened my mouth, I might have thrown up or wailed.

"That was *not* the end of the story," our father said sternly. "It was only the beginning. This went on for years, a raid here, a raid there, always ending in bloodshed. And then—"

"Oh dear," Kiandra interrupted, her voice unnaturally loud. "I think there's something wrong with our connection. The sound is going in and out. . . ."

The sound wasn't going in and out. But Kiandra reached for the computer as if she needed to fiddle with the volume control or some other setting.

"If something happens and we get cut off, remember," Enu said, "just remember, we love—"

Kiandra touched something on the keyboard, and the screen went black. Enu stopped speaking and sagged back against the couch.

"What was I saying?" he asked. "Oh, right—we don't care about you at all. You're nothing to us."

"They're so awful," Kiandra said. "Always wanting to prove their side was right in the war . . ."

My parents' image was gone, so I didn't have to look at them anymore. I still couldn't look at Kiandra or Enu. I didn't want to look at anyone or anything.

But Udans leaned down in front of us, his eyes meeting mine, and I couldn't look away. His face was as rocklike now as my father's had ever been. His scars seemed etched into his skin. My stomach heaved. Those scars probably *had* been etched into his face during the war. With a knife. Or a sword. Or bullets.

"You three are the most selfish, ungrateful children I have ever seen," he said.

Enu jumped to his feet. For a minute I thought he was going to punch Udans. Instead he just glowered at Udans, practically nose to nose.

"We don't care about our parents' stories, Udans," Enu said. "We don't care about *yours*. The past has nothing to do with us."

Kiandra grabbed my face and jerked it toward her, so she and I were eye to eye.

"Don't ask questions like that ever again," she commanded.

CHAPTER EIGHTEEN

It was nighttime, and I couldn't sleep.

I told myself it was just because I'd stayed up so late the night before and then slept until two p.m. Really it was because every time I closed my eyes, I could see my parents' anguished expressions. I could see the scars on Udans's cheek. I could see Enu face-to-face with Udans, hatred and disgust crackling between them. I could see Kiandra telling me to stop asking questions.

And, whether my eyes were open or shut, I could still hear my father saying bleakly, *They killed our people. Just because they were different. They killed my parents and grandparents. And my brothers and sisters.*

"The past has nothing to do with us," I whispered, quoting Enu. "*You're* nothing to us."

And now it was like I could hear all the Freds I'd ever known gasping at that: a son being rude and disrespectful about his parents. It seemed to go along with what Udans had said to me on our way to Ref City: *That's just how life goes* and *There's nothing you can do*. The Freds would have had fits about all of it.

Or would they? I thought, bolting upright.

My room was silent and dark and still, but my heart thudded frantically. My body seemed to think I needed to be on high alert. Enu's one line kept repeating in my head: *The past has nothing to do with us. The past has nothing to do with us.*

Was that something the Freds would actually disapprove of? Or was that one of the philosophies they lived by?

Just . . . not one they spelled out, the way they did with every single other founding principle and guiding precept?

They'd never told us about the war in Cursed Town.

They'd never explained why Rosi and I—and all the other kids younger than us—had been taken away.

They'd never told us about our ancestors. They hadn't told us my father's version of the story or Kiandra's version.

They'd never even told us their own history.

Did *they* think the past mattered?

It was a new sensation, not knowing what the Freds thought about something. The whole time I'd been growing up in Fredtown, they'd always talked and talked and talked. They'd always sounded so certain: *Edwy, this is the right way to treat other people, with respect. . . . Edwy, your education is important, so you need to do your homework. . . .*

Edwy, you need to set worthy goals, so you contribute some-thing of value to the society around you. . . . Their ideas were pounded into my brain. No matter how little attention I'd paid, I hadn't been able to avoid memorizing every word of their stupid platitudes.

How could I not know what they thought about the past?

"Rosi," I whimpered, and it was shameful to be twelve years old and sound that pathetic and desperate. But Rosi would have known the Freds' viewpoint. If she were here, I could ask her, and I would know what I wanted to think: the opposite of whatever the Freds believed.

Rosi wasn't here. Rosi was back in Cursed Town. And, unlike my parents, she didn't live in a house with a phone or a computer, where she could link in and talk to me here.

I made myself lie back down, but it was like my thoughts and questions had developed claws. They kept scratching at me, painfully. I probably wouldn't be able to sleep ever again.

I got up and walked into the living room. A tiny light gleamed in the darkness—the sleep-mode indicator on Kiandra's laptop.

Was there anything I could look up, any answer I could find online?

Without even turning on a light, I scooped up Kiandra's laptop and sank into the couch. I brought the laptop back to life, and the screen glowed at me.

I typed into the first search engine I could summon: *What do Freds believe about the past?*

The screen filled with tiny print—some professor's theories about blah-blah this and bluh-bluh that. Every word seemed to be at least six syllables long. Rosi probably would have stuck with it, stumbling her way through the thicket of nonsense, actually puzzling out its mysteries. But I stabbed my finger at the escape key.

I tried again with a different search, simply the word *Freds*.

Now the screen flooded with answers: thousands—no, millions—of results. Even a three-year-old would have been able to tell me I'd made my search too broad, but I didn't care. I clicked on the top link, figuring there had to be some reason it was the most popular. In Fredtown that would have meant it led to the most useful site.

Something like a comic strip came up. It was actually kind of funny, in a twisted way: It showed people with dead eyes and the names FRED1, FRED2, FRED3, etc., stamped across their foreheads. The Fred-zombies stole babies. They put the babies in rocket ships and flew them off into outer space.

"Yeah, right," I muttered. "As if the Freds would actually be cool enough to fly in a rocket ship. Sheesh."

I flipped to the next site, some sort of news story in tiny print.

"Snooze City," I murmured.

I was about to click out of it, but evidently I'd triggered the start of a video clip with the news story. An anchorwoman was standing in front of the biggest party I'd ever seen, in what looked to be the heart of Refuge City. People were dancing in the streets, blowing on noisemakers, setting off fireworks, and throwing handful after handful of confetti into the air.

"Here we are getting the reaction to the good news that all the human children will be returned to Earth next week," the anchorwoman said. "This is the party of the century! The party of the millennium! No—of all time! Our children are coming home!"

"What?" I whispered. "Returned to *Earth*? And . . . *human* children?"

How could there be any other type of children besides humans? Did they just mean "human," not "animal"?

The clip restarted. I scrolled down, actually reading the words of the news story. This had to be a joke. An exaggeration. A parody.

I flipped over to the next link that came up from my search, and then the next one, the next one, the next one. I let the laptop slip off my lap. I ran into Kiandra's room.

"Why didn't you or Enu tell me?" I wailed. "Why didn't anyone tell me? How could I have not known until now that Freds were aliens? And that for my entire life until two weeks ago they kidnapped every single baby born on Earth?"

CHAPTER NINETEEN

Kiandra didn't answer. I slammed my hand against the light switch on the wall, and she squinted in the sudden brightness. She pulled the covers over her face.

"How could you wake me up in the middle of the night to ask *that*?" she groaned, from beneath her blankets and sheets. "Turn off the light. Go away."

"How come you *never told me*?" I demanded, pulling her covers back, away from her face.

Kiandra winced, blinked once, and seemed to accept that I wasn't going away.

"Why was it my job?" she asked. "I never even met you until last week! I never asked for a little brother!"

That stung. But if she thought I'd get all hurt and teary-eyed and go away, she didn't know me very well.

"You're the one who wants to be the truth squad on everything!" I told her. "Our father says our ancestors were mighty travelers, you say they were poor, thieving nomads . . . that was, like, hundreds of years ago! Isn't what happened just twelve years ago more important? Isn't what happened *last week* more important? When I guess I traveled on a rocket ship from another planet and I didn't even know it? Because the Freds made us think it was just an airplane flight?"

"How was I supposed to know you were too stupid to know you'd been on a rocket ship?" Kiandra countered. She bunched up the edge of her blanket and sheet in her fists like she was about to throw them at me.

"You might have *asked*!" I snarled. "I'm your *brother*! You could have *pretended* you cared what happened to me, where I'd been, what my life was like, how I was adjusting to Ref City. . . ."

I was dangerously close to sounding like a Fred: *Families are important, and we have to watch out for one another, take care of one another. . . .* I stopped talking, but the Fred reasoning kept going in my brain: *Everyone is his or her brother's keeper. Everyone is his or her sister's keeper.*

Kiandra sat up and glared back at me.

"Did you ever wonder how it felt to me that the Freds *didn't* think I was worth rescuing?" she said. "I was *one* when you were born. Enu was three. Mother and Father sent us here when the war broke out, but we were shuffled from one bribed nanny to another. We didn't really have anyone who cared about us, unless you count Udans, and I don't. You've seen how much attention the school pays to us. How nobody's here for us even now. Did you ever look at the school website, where it says we have loving houseparents available to help us twenty-four hours a day, seven days a week—to guide us through a smooth transition to maturity?" She sounded like she was quoting. As if she'd memorized words I'd never even looked at. "But we really *don't*, because it's all lies?"

I took a step back. But then I locked my knees so she wouldn't see how badly they wanted to quiver.

"Um," I said weakly. "I thought you and Enu liked fooling our parents, and not really having to go to school."

"What other choice do we have?" she asked. "Who could get us into any kind of reputable school? *Udans?* When we're refugees from Cursed Town?"

"But—" I began.

"You think it's just about money, right?" she interrupted. Her voice was raw. "I bet you think everything should be fine for us, since our parents have so much. But let me tell you— there's not enough money in the world to make someone from Cursed Town respectable."

I hadn't been thinking about money. I'd been on the verge of quoting some Fred principle about how everyone deserved a good education. Or how everyone was equal.

But people in Ref City didn't think that way. Kiandra and Enu didn't think that way. How could I ever understand?

I remembered how my brother and sister had sounded the first day, describing our scam school. Maybe it was like how I used to brag back at the Fredtown school, *I only spent five minutes on my homework last night! Rosi, did you really spend an hour? That must mean I'm smarter than you!* When actually I was a little scared I was going to fail and be put back with the eleven-year-olds.

Bravado. That was what you called it, how Kiandra, Enu, and I all acted, most of the time. It was a way of lying and keeping secrets for all three of us.

But my waking her up in the middle of the night had scraped away Kiandra's bravado.

"You know the fighting in Cursed Town was, like, the last straw, don't you?" Kiandra asked. "What the people in Cursed Town did—that's the reason Freds came to Earth in the first place and started taking away babies. So that's why Cursed Town is the most hated place of all."

I hadn't known that. Who would have told me?

"And those Freds were supposed to be such saints," Kiandra sneered. "So compassionate and caring . . . They said their hearts were filled with wanting the very best for the human race. But how could that be? When they thought Enu and I were already so damaged at one and three that they left us behind? And they thought that only unscathed newborn human babies—babies like *you*—were worth saving?"

I had never looked at it that way. I would never in a million years have guessed that Kiandra might be jealous of my growing up in Fredtown.

"Whoa, whoa, whoa," I interrupted. "It wasn't a *good* thing to be taken to Fredtown. You got to grow up in Ref City!"

She kept glaring at me. Her words still rang in my ears: *We were shuffled from one bribed nanny to another. We didn't really have anyone who cared about us. . . . Nobody's here for us even now.*

"Anyhow, none of that is *my* fault!" I protested. "Nobody gave me a choice going to Fredtown! Nobody gave me a choice going to Cursed Town! Nobody gave me a choice coming here!"

"How many choices do you think I got?" Kiandra yelled back. "Oh, I know—do I paint my fingernails purple or blue? Do I wear a red dress or an orange one? That's all Ref City expects of me! What is my life *for*?"

"I'm here in Ref City now too," I reminded her. "What is *my* life for? Do you think *I* know?"

Once again I had Fredtown answers crowding my mind. I could have told her one of the Freds' huge founding principles was this quote from some old guy named Albert Schweitzer: *The purpose of human life is to serve, and to show compassion and the will to help others.* If Rosi had been here with us, she could have lectured Kiandra for hours about her purpose in life.

I pressed my lips together so none of those words would slip out. Especially not Rosi's name.

Enu burst into the room just then.

"What's wrong with you guys?" he asked. "The one night I go to bed early because of the big game tomorrow, you two decide three a.m. is a good time to start shouting?"

"Blame him," Kiandra said, pointing my way. "Our little brother the genius just now figured out that he lived most of his life with aliens."

Enu looked at me with what might have been a flicker of interest.

"Really?" he said. "You honestly never knew that? Didn't you ever notice how much the aliens stank?"

"Freds don't stink!" I protested automatically, almost as if he'd insulted me. I could imagine how much Rosi would laugh at the thought of me defending Freds.

I couldn't stand Freds. But it wasn't fair to say that they smelled bad. Because they didn't. They didn't smell any different from anyone else.

But they were *aliens. Aliens! From another planet! And Fredtown was on a completely different planet. . . .*

The news still seemed to be sinking in.

Maybe dull, boring, rule-bound, *safe* Fredtown had been a slightly more interesting place than I'd ever suspected.

Maybe if the Freds had ever answered any of my questions truthfully, their answers would have been kind of interesting too.

How was it possible that I'd lived with Freds my entire life, and I'd never noticed that they weren't even human?

"Did you ever see a Fred?" I asked Enu, and then Kiandra, too. "Did you ever smell one?"

Kiandra sniffed.

"How would we know?" she asked. "Rumor was, the Freds who came here to steal babies always looked exactly like humans. They were in disguise. That's probably why some *ignorant* people"—she shot a glance at Enu—"started saying you could smell them."

"If you think about it, how do we even know that you're not really some Fred-child sent here to take over our planet?" Enu challenged me. "How do we know that *you're* really human?"

"Because I look like you!" I said, and it was weird, how panicked my voice sounded. What would Enu do if he talked himself into the idea that I was a Fred? "Kiandra says I'm your mini-me!"

"Freds could have faked that," Enu said, "if they can fake looking human."

Something clicked in my brain.

"Tug on my face," I told Enu.

"What?"

He sounded so surprised, I decided he'd never really thought I was a Fred. Maybe he didn't have that much imagination. Or maybe . . . maybe he had started thinking of me as his little brother.

But I took a step toward Enu and tilted my chin up.

"You pull on my face, see if it comes off," I said. "Because . . . one time in Fredtown, I kind of . . . kicked at my Fred-father's jaw. I was just goofing around. But the way I hit him, it made something happen to his face. . . ."

"*What* happened to his face?" It didn't surprise me that Kiandra was the one who asked, the one who actually sounded curious, while Enu backed away from me.

"It was like for just an instant I could see . . . fur," I said. "*Bluish* fur. But he turned away from me, and it was over so fast that I was never really sure. . . ."

I didn't tell them the rest of the story, which was that I'd gone to Rosi for help figuring out exactly what I'd seen, and she'd gotten mad at me. She'd accused me of just wanting to get her into the same kind of trouble I was in.

It was true that I was always in trouble in Fredtown. But I swear, I hadn't wanted to make problems for Rosi. Not then, anyway. I'd just wanted answers.

My mind darted away from the memory, just like it'd been darting away from just about every memory I'd had of Rosi ever since I'd gotten to Ref City.

"Look," I begged Enu, grabbing his hand and slamming it up against my face. "Pull. Prove to yourself that I'm human."

He shoved me away instead.

"I know you're human," he mumbled. "I was just messing with you."

Kiandra pulled her tablet computer out of the folds of her bedding. She had spare computers stashed around the apartment the same way Enu had spare video games everywhere.

"Look," she said, typing something quickly and then holding the tablet out to me. "This is what Freds really look like, out of their disguises."

The picture on the screen was blurry and distant. I saw a creature with fur—blue? Green? Turquoise? The longer I looked, the more trouble I had deciding how to describe it. I also couldn't quite tell how many eyes and noses and mouths I was seeing. The undisguised Fred looked . . . soft. That was all.

"How do you know that's a real Fred?" I asked Kiandra. "Why didn't I find any images like that when I was searching before? Is that the best picture you can find? It's awfully fuzzy."

"It's something about how the light hits their fur—supposedly they're hard for humans to see clearly," Kiandra said. "That *is* the best picture out there. That's why, on the intergalactic court, things are set up so that each planetary species sees every other species as some version of themselves. Our human representatives look around and see nothing but other humans. I guess the Freds look around and see every other species looking like Freds. It's like how the United Nations used to arrange to have simultaneous translations so that people from every nation heard the people of every other nation just speaking their language."

I almost dropped the tablet. Kiandra, with her advanced

sense of what was best for electronics, pulled it out of my hands.

"There's an entire—what'd you call it—an intergalactic court?" I repeated numbly. "So are there more species besides just Freds and humans? Why isn't everybody talking about this all the time? Why aren't we constantly sending out rocket ships from Ref City to, to . . . ?"

I wanted to say, *Why didn't humans built a rocket ship to rescue me and the other kids from Fredtown? Why didn't humans get revenge on Freds by turning around and kidnapping Fred-kids?*

But I didn't even know if there was such a thing as Fred-kids.

There were evidently a million things I didn't know.

Kiandra snapped the cover over the face of the tablet.

"Humans haven't exactly had a good experience, interacting with alien species," she muttered. "It's like, everybody would just rather not think about it. Or talk about it."

Enu flashed me the confident smile he used on the basketball court.

"Why think about unpleasant things you can't do anything about?" he asked. "Why waste time on that, when you can play video games or basketball, and just have fun?"

CHAPTER TWENTY

Why think about unpleasant things you can't do anything about?

Don't ask questions like that ever again.

The past has nothing to do with us.

That's just how life goes.

There's nothing you can do.

My brain would not shut down. It still wanted to figure out something I could do. It kept racing through the same path of thoughts as if eventually the path would lead somewhere new.

Kiandra had kicked me out of her room. Enu had given me strict orders not to make another sound the rest of the night. Now I was back in my own room, back in my own bed, back with a racing mind that wouldn't let me sleep. Kiandra and Enu and the computer had just given me more to think about, more to keep me awake.

Rosi, wherever you are back in Cursed Town—has anyone told you that Freds are aliens? How did you handle the news?

What did you decide to do about it? Is there anything anyone can do?

Okay, that was new. This was the first time my brain had started acting like it could communicate directly with Rosi, across the many, many kilometers that separated us.

I *ached* to talk with Rosi.

For the past week and a half I'd managed to distract myself every time some thought of her had entered my brain. It was like I'd boxed up everything about her in some imaginary vault. But now it was like that vault had sprung a leak.

Or just cracked open completely.

I couldn't stop thinking about Rosi. The way she looked at me. The way, even when she was mad at me, she still worried about me.

The Freds always looked at you that way too, my brain reminded me.

But there was a difference. It was like the Freds *had* to look at me that way. They were adults. They were Freds. They just weren't capable of looking at kids with disgust or hatred in their eyes.

With Rosi it was different. It was like . . . like she *chose* to care about me.

But that had never stopped her from being furious with me. Back in Fredtown she'd constantly gotten mad at me for asking questions.

No, not for asking questions, my conscience forced me to admit. *For being rude to the Freds in how I asked the questions.*

But once we were back in our parents' hometown, in Cursed Town, she had asked rude questions too. That day when she found me fishing—because my parents were punishing me—she, not I, had been the one to ask, *Doesn't it seem like every adult we've ever known is hiding something?*

It *had* seemed like that. And she was right: Everyone had been hiding something.

The Freds had been hiding the fact that they were aliens.

Our real parents had been hiding the news of the war that had ended the day Rosi and I were born.

My real parents had also hidden the fact that they were going to send me to Refuge City. They'd hidden that news practically right up until the moment they did it.

They'd hidden the news that I had an older brother and sister, too.

And they'd hidden the fact that they were essentially prisoners trapped in Cursed Town, never allowed to leave.

Was that everything? Were those all the secrets Rosi and I had missed?

Oh, Rosi, I thought. *What if we'd been able to find answers together? Would you right now be explaining to me how all of this makes sense? How it fits with a saintly, Fred-logical way of seeing the universe?*

I would never in a million years have admitted this to Rosi, but without her I was totally confused. I couldn't make sense of anything I'd discovered.

Freds are aliens. Humans who are alive right now have been in wars. War isn't something that only happened centuries and centuries ago, before humans were civilized. There's an intergalactic court out there somewhere that, that . . .

My brain made a little leap. This was like standing before a box of dumped-out puzzle pieces and suddenly seeing how two of the pieces fit together.

On the so-called "plane" that had brought Rosi and me and the other kids from Fredtown to Cursed Town—an "airplane" that I now knew was actually a rocket ship—there had been men who'd ordered us around and were mean to the Freds. Those men weren't Freds, but something had been a little off about them, too. In fact I'd been so certain something was wrong with them that I had scratched words into my seat on the plane—er, rocket ship—saying that they weren't real. That day, that was all I'd been able to manage.

What if those men had been from the intergalactic court? They'd waved around a decree telling the Freds they couldn't come on the "plane" with us. What if that decree was from the intergalactic court too?

Didn't "intergalactic court" sound like some group that would tell people from lots of different planets what to do?

"Ro—" I actually started to call out for Rosi, as if she were right there and could confirm that what I'd figured out was right.

I paused, remembering how mad Enu would get if I woke him again. I listened hard, but all I could hear was the distant hum of our refrigerator, out in the kitchen.

"Never mind," I muttered.

I focused on the refrigerator hum, thinking maybe it would lull me to sleep.

No luck. I couldn't even shut my eyes without them popping right back open a second later.

I slipped out of bed again and started pacing. My room wasn't that big—I could go only five steps in any direction before I had to turn around and walk back the other way. I might have managed six steps before turning around if it hadn't been for the TV where Enu played his favorite video game, the one about destroying spaceships.

Spaceships. Rocket ships. Same thing.

Another puzzle piece fell into place. Maybe.

What if it's not just a coincidence that that game is about spaceships? I wondered. *What if Enu and Kiandra— and all the other kids who were too old to be kidnapped by the Freds . . . What if they all hate us younger kids so much that they* wish *they could have destroyed the rocket ships that brought us home?*

I gagged. I had to stop pacing for a moment and hold on to the wall.

I remembered the video clip of how much Refuge City had celebrated the news that the human children would be coming home.

Then I remembered that Enu had called the spaceship video game "old." He'd had it for years.

That video game wasn't about humans hating humans. It was about how much humans wished they could have destroyed the spaceships that had brought Freds and other aliens to Earth in the first place.

I stopped gagging. But I kept hanging on to the wall.

Humans wanted to kill Freds and other aliens, but they could only pretend to do it, in a game, I realized.

Humans had flying cars and computers and athletic domes that seemed to float above the ground. Freds had the ability to make themselves look like an entirely different species. They had spaceships that could look like airplanes. They had the ability to trick human children into thinking they were on Earth, when they were really on an entirely different planet. They had the ability to steal every human child born on Earth for twelve years, and humans hadn't been able to stop them until . . . well, I guessed it wasn't until the intergalactic court got involved.

Freds were superior to humans.

In my mind I could hear Rosi arguing, *Well, yes. Of course. Freds are peaceful and kind. And humans were still fighting wars just twelve years ago. . . .*

"Oh, stuff it, Rosi," I said aloud, and in that moment I didn't care if Enu heard and woke up and got mad.

But *would* Rosi still argue that Freds were so great?

In my mind I saw the celebrations in the video clip of when Refuge City got the news that all the human children were coming back to Earth. I saw all the confetti swirling in the air. I saw all the pain the Freds had caused, being undone.

"You're not that special after all, Rosi," I whispered. "Neither am I."

She and I had been the oldest kids in our Fredtown, the only ones removed from Cursed Town the very day the war ended, the day we were born. But I knew now from my online research that there had been lots and lots of Fredtowns: at least one for every village and town and city on Earth. Refuge City had gotten its kids back too. Refuge City was a lot bigger than Cursed Town; there were probably dozens of twelve-year-olds like Rosi and me who had come back here. Maybe I'd even passed some of them on the street. Like me, they were probably just lying low. Not talking about Freds or Fredtown, because it stirred up lots of bad memories for everyone older than us.

I let go of the wall and reached for the doorknob.

If I couldn't talk to Rosi right now, at least I could find and talk to some other kid my age who'd been raised by Freds.

He or she could help me figure things out just as well as Rosi would.

Anyone raised by Freds would want to help.

Right?

CHAPTER
TWENTY-ONE

It was five a.m. now, and I was staring at a sign that said
SOUP KITCHEN.

Without waking up Enu—or, more important, Kiandra—
I'd had to rely on my own computer skills to find any information about other kids raised by Freds who were now in
Refuge City. Maybe the Freds hadn't taught me very good
computer-research skills; maybe they had tried and I just
hadn't listened. Whatever the reason, I'd had to search and
search and search. And I'd found only one clue: a mysterious
online posting that said, *Seeking: Refuge City kids who want
to talk about how to adapt to our new homes.*

That had to be from some kid or kids who had a new
home because their last home was with Freds. Didn't it?

What else could it be?

The last part of that post said, *If you meet this description,
come to 9405 Bull Wallow Road and ask for Z.*

It sounded like the setup for a prank. Maybe the kind of
prank *I* might have pulled back in Fredtown. Like, I might

walk into this 9405 Bull Wallow Road and get a pie in the face. If there had been any other lead online—or if I'd been patient enough to wait until Kiandra woke up so I could ask for help, and if *she'd* found something—I would have ignored this posting.

But as it was, I'd left the apartment and walked straight to 9405 Bull Wallow Road.

And . . . it was a soup kitchen. Whatever that was.

Probably just someplace that serves soup, I told myself. *That's okay. I had a long walk, and I'm hungry.*

Soup for breakfast was a little unusual, but I didn't care.

A broken shutter banged against the window frame of the next building over, and I shivered. The area around Bull Wallow Road did not look like any of the other glitzy, shiny new areas I'd seen everywhere else I'd been in Refuge City. It didn't look like Fredtown, either. It looked old and broken-down and shadowy.

It looked a lot like the worst areas I'd seen in Cursed Town.

It's just . . . not quite sunrise yet, I told myself. *That's all. This area will look fine once the sun's up.*

That gave me the courage to knock at the door of the soup kitchen.

"Come on in!" someone yelled from inside. "Coffee's almost ready! So's breakfast!"

I pushed my way in to find a long, narrow room full of rickety tables and mismatched chairs. Most of the chairs were empty, but a few contained hunched-over shapes—old men? Old women? It was hard to tell. They all seemed to be gray-haired and grizzled and snoring.

I looked around for the person who'd yelled "Come in!" I caught a flicker of movement from the far end of the room— it was a man standing behind a counter.

"Are you hungry?" the man asked gently.

"No," I said, because suddenly I wasn't.

"That's fine," the man said, but he sounded like he didn't believe me.

"I'm here to see Z," I said.

His friendly expression tightened.

"Do you know her?" he asked. "Does she know you?"

Her? I thought. *She?*

"No," I admitted, because I didn't think I could bluff my way through this one. "I just saw something she posted online. I wanted to . . . talk about adjusting to our new homes."

Now the man spoke through clenched teeth.

"I don't really think that's—" he began.

But a door banged behind him, and a short girl with reddish-brown pigtails pushed past him.

"Is it—" she began eagerly. Her gaze fell on me and she looked confused. "Oh. I thought . . . I don't know you."

The man put his hand on the girl's shoulder.

"We can ask him to leave, Zeebs," he said. "We have a standing arrangement with the police, if anyone causes a disturbance here . . ."

This was *so* annoying.

"I'm not causing a disturbance!" I insisted. "This girl—Zeebs?—she pretty much invited me here, saying to come here and ask for Z if I wanted to talk about adapting to my new home. I'm just doing what she told me to do!"

The girl narrowed her eyes at me. They were so light, they were almost gold.

"Prove you grew up in a Fredtown," she whispered.

I sighed.

"A founding principle of Fredtown," I said. "*The purpose of human life is to serve, and to show compassion and the will to help others. Another one: The only thing we have to fear is fear itself. And another one: No one is to be called an enemy. And . . .*"

I hoped the girl didn't notice I was mostly going for the short ones. She was making me nervous. And I had tried really, really hard the whole time I lived in Fredtown not to memorize anything.

And . . . what if different Fredtowns had had different founding principles?

The girl took a step away from the father and closer to me.

"Daddy, it's okay," she said. "He may not have grown up in the same Fredtown as me, but he did grow up in a Fredtown."

"And you think that makes him trustworthy?" he asked doubtfully.

"Yes," the girl said.

She stepped out from behind the counter and put her hand on my arm, guiding me toward one of the tables in the corner, away from any of the gray, hunched-over people.

"Daddy, we'll just be sitting right over here," she said. "Nothing's going to happen."

The man frowned but didn't stop us. He went back to making coffee.

The girl and I sat down on opposite sides of the small table, and suddenly I felt a little tongue-tied. For much of the past year I hadn't even been able to talk to Rosi without making her mad, and she and I had known each other our whole lives.

"Are you sure you don't want to have me prove I live in Refuge City now?" I asked. "Because that's what you were looking for, right—other kids from Refuge City?"

"I was looking for other kids who grew up in Fredtowns," she said firmly. "Other kids my age. But . . . if you had to, how would you prove you live in Refuge City?"

I thought about that one. As far as I could tell, Refuge

City didn't have precepts or founding principles. Unless it was one of the things Udans or Enu had told me: *Why think about unpleasant things you can't do anything about?* And, *The past has nothing to do with us.* And, *That's just how life goes. There's nothing you can do.*

But what if I was wrong, and the girl didn't recognize any of those?

Suddenly I knew what I should say.

"I like your freckles," I told her. "But . . . I'm not going to say anything about the fact that your skin is paler than mine. I'm not even going to notice it. Uh-uh. Can't even see it."

The girl laughed.

"That is how everybody acts in Refuge City!" she agreed. "They talk about how people look all the time. But they're scared to say anything about the color of people's skin. Even though really everyone now is just various shades of brown. Because that's one of the things that people used to fight about all the time."

I hadn't known that.

"Skin color?" I asked. "Really? They fought about that? Why? Who cares?"

The girl shrugged.

"My parents say it's all because of history. History we never learned in our Fredtowns." She stuck out her hand and shook mine. "I'm Zeba."

"Edwy," I told her. "It's good to be around someone who remembers what it was like to be raised by crazy Freds!"

Zeba bit her lip and pulled her hand back.

"I never thought they were crazy," she said. "It's not crazy to be . . . idealistic."

"You're like my friend Rosi, then," I said. "That's what she believed too. Back in Fredtown, she always thought that the Freds were right. And . . . that I was wrong."

And even though I'd told myself that was what I was looking for—someone like Rosi, someone who'd explain things to me in a Rosi kind of way—my heart sank a little.

Maybe I'd really wanted to find someone who would see everything the same way I did.

Zeba toyed with the rubber band at the end of one of her braids.

"Some would say my real parents and the Freds aren't a whole lot different," she said. "Daddy and Mama—they came to Refuge City twenty years ago when it was mostly just a processing center for refugees from all the wars. Before all the fancy buildings. Before all the rich people came. My real parents like to help people, just like the Freds do. But . . . they're angry."

"Angry?" I repeated numbly. "Your parents are angry?"

I had a hard time imagining anyone who was like the Freds being angry.

Zeba nodded, her braids thumping her shoulders.

"They say the Freds never understood human nature," she whispered. She glanced over her shoulder, back toward the man in the kitchen. "They say taking every kid away and then bringing us back twelve years later made all of Earth into a powder keg. And . . . I think they're mad that even good people like them had their kids taken away. My parents call themselves humanitarians. All they've done their whole lives is help people. They think that they—and everyone else like them—should have been allowed to keep their own children all along. They say it's not fair that they were punished for what other humans did."

"Oh," I said, blinking at her. *Powder keg? Humanitarians?* These were new words for me, new thoughts. I'd been wrong: Talking to Zeba wasn't like talking to Rosi. Rosi and I were connected. Zeba was a stranger. I didn't understand her; she didn't understand me.

"But do your parents think the Freds were right to take kids away from *some* people?" I asked. "From *bad* people?"

Zeba tilted her head. Now her braids looked crooked.

"What do *you* think?" she asked. "Should kids be forced to grow up with parents who maybe don't even love them? Who don't raise them in a loving way? Who might even teach them bad things?"

I thought about my own parents, who were thieves. Who'd

let me think I'd been kidnapped. Who'd sent me away.

But only to get me away from Cursed Town, I told myself. *They think I'm getting a good education in Ref City.*

It was weird how much I longed to defend my parents. I wanted to ask Zeba, *How bad is too bad? Do parents have to be perfect, or else?*

What if it's a lot harder for some people to be good than it is for others?

I couldn't say those words out loud.

"Why did you put that thing online?" I asked Zeba instead. "Why did you ask kids to come here if they wanted to talk about adjusting to their new homes?"

Zeba looked down at her hands, neatly folded in her lap.

"Mama and Daddy say, in the current political climate it's best not to say too much about Freds or Fredtown," she explained. "They say people want to forget all that. But kids raised by Freds want to help people. It's what we grew up with. Lots of places in Refuge City, no one wants to help anyone. I thought if kids came to the soup kitchen, they could help poor people, and it would make them feel . . . needed. Right again. Normal. Useful."

I jerked back, my knee jarring against the table.

"So you were just looking for kids to help you and your parents in their . . . their business?" I accused.

"Our soup kitchen isn't a business," Zeba said. "It's a

charity. We give out food for free. People need this soup kitchen or they would starve, because there's corruption— the money these old people should get to live on goes into building newer and fancier sports arenas and, and—"

Her father suddenly appeared behind her and put a hand on her shoulder.

"Zeba, is it time to ask this boy to leave?" he said. "If he's starting to get violent and yelling at you, then—"

"I'm not yelling!" Okay, I did kind of yell that. And maybe I'd been a little loud saying that thing about her parents' business.

I realized that some of the sleeping old, gray people had awakened and were staring over at us, blinking in confusion. I lowered my voice.

"Anyhow, I am definitely not being *violent*," I told Zeba's father. "I just proved I was raised by Freds, remember? Freds didn't let us learn anything about violence!"

I thought guiltily about the video games Enu had taught me, and the way I'd learned to cheat on the basketball court. Then I pushed that out of my mind and looked back at Zeba. She had tears glistening in her gold eyes now, but I was too mad to care.

"I thought you said your parents were 'humanitarians,'" I snapped at her. "I thought you said they liked to help people. And *this* is how they treat people like me? Is it because I was raised by Freds? Is it because I'm from a different Fredtown than yours? What's the problem?"

Zeba's father let his shoulders sag. His hand clenched on Zeba's shoulder.

"I—" he began. "I'm sorry. I never realized how hard it would be, having an almost-teenage daughter. I just want to protect her. And you kids from Fredtowns, you don't have any sense of the dangers around you. It's like Zeba is defenseless."

"Daddy, I can take care of myself," Zeba said. She sounded embarrassed.

"Anyway," Zeba's father said. "Let me begin again. I'm Michael." He reached out and shook my hand. "I've been given to understand that there were twelve Fredtowns associated with kids from Refuge City, because the Freds preferred to raise children in smaller communities. Which Fredtown were you in? Are you friends with any of the other kids I've met through Zeba? Friends with any of the other kids who have already started volunteering here?"

Ugh. So Zeba had been right—other kids raised by Freds *had* wanted to work in this soup kitchen. They still wanted to help other people and live by Fred principles even though they were back on Earth.

I suddenly felt like shocking this smug, Fred-like man. Udans, Enu, and Kiandra wouldn't have approved, but I intended to enjoy telling him where I was really from.

"Actually," I said, "I didn't grow up in any of the Fredtowns connected to Refuge City. *My* Fredtown was the one with kids from Cursed Town. And when I went home from

Fredtown, that's where I went first. Cursed Town. That's where *I* belong."

Zeba's father surprised me by letting go of Zeba's shoulder and wrapping his arms around me instead, in a giant hug.

"You survived! You escaped! Then there *are* still refugees getting out of Cursed Town! Hallelujah!" he cried. "Tell me—how did you get away from the fighting?"

This man was every bit as crazy as a Fred.

I pulled away from his hug.

"Um . . . the Freds kidnapped me the day I was born, just like everyone else kidnapped by a Fred," I muttered. "It *was* the last day of the war, and—"

"No, I don't mean twelve years ago," Zeba's father said impatiently. "I mean last week when the fighting started again and they imposed martial law. But you escaped?"

I didn't know what "martial law" meant. I barely understood the word "fighting." But I twisted up out of my chair and faced the man. I grabbed the front of his shirt.

"There was fighting in Cursed Town last week?" I asked. "People got hurt there *last week*?"

The man's expression softened. His eyes filled with an expression I recognized from every single time my Fredparents had ever glanced at me. Sympathy. Pity. Sorrow.

"Yes," he whispered. "There was fighting in Cursed Town last week. And people were hurt. People were killed."

"Rosi," I said. "Rosi, Rosi, Rosi, Rosi . . ."

CHAPTER TWENTY-TWO

I was lucky there was a computer in the back office of the soup kitchen. Or maybe the people at the soup kitchen were lucky, because I might have started throwing tables and chairs and turning the whole building upside down looking for a computer, if Zeba and her father hadn't immediately grasped that I needed one.

"We can look up the names of the dead and the injured," Zeba's father said, leading me back toward the office and the computer. "And the names of the imprisoned combatants . . . I'm sure it will turn out that your friend is fine. A kid raised by Freds wouldn't have been part of a battle. I take it you got out of Cursed Town before the fighting began?"

He was treating me like an invalid, like someone who might not even be able to stand up by himself.

Back in Fredtown, I'd always hated how my Fred-parents babied me when I was sick. But now . . .

Maybe I really wouldn't be able to stand up if Zeba's dad wasn't holding on to me.

The soup kitchen's computer was ancient and clunky and huge, and it seemed to take a year to boot up.

"Let's see, the news coverage here was . . . suppressed," Zeba's father said, leaning over the keyboard. "Most people in Refuge City just want to hear sports scores and entertainment news. But some of the more serious news sites devoted a lot of time to this disaster. . . ."

"Something that happened in tiny little Cursed Town was that awful?" I whispered numbly, even as I sank into a chair. "Awful enough that people in Refuge City noticed?"

People who weren't Enu, Kiandra, and me, anyway. Or Enu's basketball-playing friends. I thought about my parents' expressions when they'd assured Enu, Kiandra, and me that they were "thriving" in Cursed Town and everything was fine. They'd known about the fighting.

They'd known that they could get away with lying to us.

Zeba patted my shoulder from behind, but I didn't look back at her. I kept my eyes glued to the computer screen.

Her father paused in his typing.

"The fighting in Refuge City set off . . . repercussions for the entire planet," he said. "I think the newscasters can explain it better than I can. This is from last week, the first announcement."

He hit the enter key, and a grim-looking woman appeared on the screen. She had on a frilly blouse and a bright gold suit. Her hair was stiff as a helmet, as if someone had spent hours turning it into an architectural structure. But her face sagged, and her skin had a grayish tint that made me think of dismay and distress. She looked as hopeless as the old people waiting out in the dining area of the soup kitchen.

"This is hard news to impart," she said. "We've just learned that events in Cursed Town this afternoon have triggered the most controversial aspects of Agreement 5062."

Someone gasped behind her in the news studio. Or maybe I let out a gasp myself.

"Agreement 5062?" I repeated. "I've heard of that. On the plane—or rocket ship—coming from Fredtown. That was the agreement that said none of the Freds were allowed to come home with us. And that the men who did bring us home—they had to leave, like, twenty minutes after dropping us off. . . ."

"That was only one part of Agreement 5062," Zeba's dad said. "The whole agreement had all the details about what would happen when you children came home. And . . . about what would happen if there was any fighting after you got home."

"As of this afternoon, the Enforcers have returned," the newscaster said. "I repeat, the aliens known as Enforcers are back on Earth because of fighting in Cursed Town. They are in charge. For now they hold control only in the restricted regions around Cursed Town, but if any fighting spreads, they will expand the territory under their control."

I didn't know what—or who—Enforcers were, so her words just flowed over me. I wanted to complain, *Can't we just get to the lists of the injured and dead?* But I wasn't sure I could say the word "dead" out loud.

And, anyhow, the newscaster was saying, "Here's video we've obtained of the fighting today."

Her face disappeared, replaced by grainy footage of a scruffy-looking marketplace.

"Oh! That's the marketplace in Cursed Town!" I cried. My heart thudded hard; I remembered that the day Rosi had found me fishing in Cursed Town's creek, she'd been on her way to see her father in the marketplace. She'd been taking him lunch.

And then she was supposed to spend all afternoon with him selling apples.

But I saw her after that, that night! I reminded myself. *I know she stayed safe that afternoon!*

I just didn't know what had happened to her the next afternoon. Or the next one. Or the one after that.

Or, for that matter, I didn't know if she'd gotten home safely the night we'd both sneaked out. The night I was kidnapped.

The night I'd avoided thinking about for a week and a half.

"What day was this?" I asked Zeba's dad, even as the scene

on the screen flashed around aimlessly, showing peaches, cassava root, and bags of rice, all laid out on tables for sale.

"Monday a week ago," he said distantly, his eyes on the screen.

The day after I'd been kidnapped. The day after my parents had sent me away because . . . . because they knew no one was safe in Cursed Town?

Or because they knew the fighting was coming?

Someone darted across the screen—a girl carrying a small boy piggyback-style.

"Oh! There's my friend Rosi! With her brother Bobo! She's safe!"

I didn't hear if Zeba or her father answered, because I was watching Rosi so intently.

Rosi scrambled up on top of a table. That was not very Rosi-like. If I'd done something like that, Rosi would have scolded me, *No, Edwy, don't! It doesn't look very safe. You might get hurt. You might ruin the goods someone has for sale.*

What had happened to Rosi to make her desperate enough to act like me?

A close-up of Rosi's face appeared. She seemed to be shouting something, but I couldn't hear what it was. Instead the newscaster's voice apologized, "Unfortunately we only have visuals of this, not audio."

"She's probably telling everyone to be peaceful and calm

and nice to everyone," I told Zeba and her father. "That's how Rosi is."

In the next instant someone punched Rosi in the stomach.

"No!" I screamed. "No, no—"

Rosi, with Bobo still on her back, doubled over and wobbled at the edge of the table.

"Somebody help her!" I screamed, as if I were right there and everything was happening right now.

Hands reached up for Rosi, but no one steadied her. No one soothed her or gently helped her and Bobo down, like any Fred would have done.

Instead these hands yanked her off the table, and slammed her and Bobo toward the ground.

"What? Who does that to *Rosi*?" I cried.

On the screen people crowded around her and Bobo. I saw someone lift Bobo and pull him away from the throng, but Rosi didn't stand up. Nobody helped *her*. And even though Bobo screamed and held out his hands toward where Rosi had fallen, people kept passing Bobo farther and farther away from his sister.

"Zeba, you don't have to watch anymore," I heard Zeba's father say. I realized she was crying behind me.

Zeba's father reached for the keyboard, as if he intended to shut everything down. I grabbed his hand and shoved it away.

"I have to see what happened next," I insisted, and Zeba's father drew his hand back.

I was watching for Rosi so intently, it took me a moment to realize that lots of people had started hitting each other. A man picked up a kitchen knife from one of the tables and started brandishing it.

And then everything swayed and went black, as if the camera filming the scene had fallen to the ground.

The newscaster in the gold jacket appeared on the screen again.

"Unfortunately, that's all the footage we were able to retrieve," she said.

I looked to Zeba's father.

"You said there were lists," I hissed, as if I was accusing him of something. "Lists of the injured and the dead. Is Rosi . . . Is Rosi . . . ?"

"What's your friend's last name?" he asked.

Oddly, I had to think hard about that. Even back in Fredtown I'd made a big deal about having people call me Edwy Watanaboneset, my full name. I'd liked every single one of those syllables. But Rosi had laughed at that. She'd been the only Rosi around, so she didn't see why people had to waste their time saying her first and last name. But of course I knew what her last name was.

"Alvaran," I said. "She's Rosi Alvaran."

Zeba's father didn't answer, but quietly typed something into the computer.

"She's not on the list of the dead," he said, and I let out a breath I hadn't realized I'd been holding. "She isn't on the list of the hospitalized."

Well, there. Everything was fine. Rosi was okay.

But Zeba's father was still typing. Something else came up on the screen, and he sat back so he didn't block my view. But my eyes were too blurry to focus. I could only stare.

"Your friend Rosi was thrown into prison as one of the combatants," he said.

Combatants? Combat? People who fight?

"That can't be!" I protested. "Rosi wouldn't fight! Who would put Rosi in prison? That's got to be a mistake! Someone needs to fix this—of course Rosi's innocent!"

Zeba's father peered at me, and it was awful how much pity his gaze contained.

"Regardless," he said. "She *was* in prison. But . . . she escaped. And nobody knows where she is now."

CHAPTER TWENTY-THREE

I tore back into my own apartment.

"Kiandra!" I screamed. "Kiandra, you have to help me!"

I'd run all the way home from the soup kitchen. My breath came in ragged gasps, and after I swung the door open, banging it against the wall, I had to stop for a minute to lean over and try to inhale.

The apartment was silent and almost as dark as when I'd left it two hours—and a lifetime—ago.

"Kiandra?" I called again.

A bedroom door creaked open—not Kiandra's, but Enu's.

Oh, yeah, the whole "Don't you dare wake me until morning" threat . . . I guess this isn't really what Enu would call morning yet. . . .

I didn't care if I made him mad. Not when Rosi was missing.

But when he stepped out of his room, he wasn't rubbing sleep out of his eyes or balling his hands into fists. He was already dressed, in his blue basketball warm-up suit, his orange basketball T-shirt peeking out from underneath. The front of his hair looked damp, as if he'd splashed it while washing his face.

"Edwy, where have you been?" he asked. "Why aren't you ready? It's almost time to leave for the big game!"

"What?" It took me a ridiculous amount of time to remember that a basketball game was the reason he'd been so upset about me disturbing his sleep in the middle of the night. "Oh—the game. I can't go. I've got to get Kiandra to help me find my friend Rosi. She's missing. Kiandra can hack into any computer and find out anything she wants, can't she? Can't she?"

That was the hope I'd been holding on to, all the way from the soup kitchen.

"Rosi? Who's Rosi?" Enu squinched up his face into his most annoyed expression. "How important can this friend be if I've never heard you mention her even once, the whole time you've lived here?"

So important that I was afraid to mention her name to you even once, the whole time I've lived here, I thought. *Because if I talked about her, that would remind me I left her behind. . . .*

To Enu, I just said, "More important than a basketball game!"

Dimly, behind me, I heard the ding of the elevator. Had

Kiandra gotten up early and gone out on some errand? And was she just now coming back?

I turned around to look, through the apartment doorway. The elevator doors parted, revealing a girl standing there, looking around. It wasn't Kiandra. It was Zeba.

"You followed me?" I asked, puzzled.

"You ran out of the soup kitchen in such a panic," she said. "I wanted to make sure you were all right."

"Of course I'm not all right!" I yelled at her. "My friend is missing!"

Enu put his hands on my shoulder.

"Dude, get ahold of yourself," he said. "Go get changed. Whoever this Rosi is, you can look for her after the game. It'll probably turn out she's not even missing. She's just not talking to you right now. Girls do that sometimes. Especially the pretty ones." He gave a teasing grin. "I didn't know there was some babe you were sweet on—"

I shook his hands off my shoulder.

"She *is* missing, and I'm *not* going to the game!" I insisted.

Finally, finally, Kiandra's door creaked open.

"What is wrong with the two of you?" she demanded. "Yelling *again*?" Her sharp eyes fell on Zeba. "And you have friends over?"

"Hi, I'm—" Zeba started to say, stepping forward with her hand outstretched. But Kiandra ignored her, and so did I.

"This is an emergency," I told Kiandra, rushing to her side. I grabbed her laptop from the couch as I passed it, and I flipped the screen open to face her. "You've got to help me! Log on now!"

Kiandra yawned.

"And people always say *girls* are overdramatic," she muttered, rolling her eyes in Zeba's general direction. She turned her attention back to me. "Squirt, I don't know what your problem is, but did you ever think that maybe I already have plans for the day? Why would what *you* want automatically be more important than what *I* want?"

"See, Kiandra's not going to help you," Enu said. "You should have known she's too mean for that. But today that's good, because now you'll go to the basketball game with me."

He took two quick steps across the room and grabbed the back of my sweatshirt hood, tugging me toward the door. I jerked away from him.

"What? You want me to beg?" Enu asked. "Edwy, we need you to have enough players."

What was wrong with Enu and Kiandra? No kid had ever gone missing in Fredtown—of course not—but if anyone had, everyone in town would have instantly dropped everything and searched and searched and searched until the kid was found. Back in Fredtown everyone in town would drop everything and come to the rescue if a kid so much as scraped a knee.

Enu and Kiandra wouldn't even listen to me. Not really.

Who would have thought I'd ever miss anything about Fredtown?

"I'm trying to find a missing friend, and you think I'm going to stop just to play a *game*?" I asked Enu. His eyes held so much surprise, I thought, *Well, what else would he expect? Haven't I just been playing games ever since I got to Ref City? Even when I knew Rosi* might *be in danger?*

I remembered the grainy video I'd seen, the punch landing in Rosi's stomach. This was different. Now I *knew* something awful had happened to her.

"And all you care about is your basketball team having enough players?" I kept ranting to Enu. "Find some other warm body to sit on the bench for you!"

"Look, if *you* help Edwy," Zeba said to Kiandra, "I'll take Edwy's place in that basketball game."

Enu snapped his attention back to the doorway, where Zeba was standing.

"You're a girl!" he said.

"Girls can play basketball too!" Kiandra snarled at him.

Would you all just stop talking about basketball? And what girls can or can't do? I wanted to explode. *We have to look for Rosi!*

But I saw something in how Kiandra straightened up, glaring at Enu.

Maybe, maybe . . .

"I *will* help Edwy," Kiandra decided, lifting her chin

defiantly. "So . . . oh, sorry, Enu, looks like you really will have to let a girl play on your team."

Had Kiandra maybe wanted to play with Enu and his friends sometime, and he hadn't asked her because she was a girl? How crazy would that be?

"But—" Enu began.

"Or if you've got some other friend you want to ask instead, I don't mind," Zeba said, Fred-like generosity in her voice.

"Enu *doesn't* have any other friends he could ask, or he wouldn't have asked Edwy in the first place," Kiandra said. She leaned back against her doorway and grinned. She was enjoying this moment way too much.

Can't we just focus on Rosi? I wanted to scream. But . . . it kind of seemed like I needed to get Enu to accept Zeba on his basketball team first.

Enu looked Zeba up and down. If it'd been me, I would have stood up straight and tried to look taller—and scrappier, because I'd learned that that mattered in Ref City. But Zeba only gave him a kind, friendly, Fred-like smile.

"Are you as good as Edwy is at cheating?" Enu asked, and I cringed.

"No," Zeba said, shaking her head firmly. "I don't cheat. That would be against the rules."

Growing up in a Fredtown really had ruined her.

"But she's got a great jump shot," I said quickly, making up something, anything, as well as I could. "It's, like, a thousand times better than mine."

Zeba's pale eyebrows shot up.

"Edwy, that's not—" she began.

Before she could finish on the word "true," I quickly added, "And she's a great team player. Everything Zeba does is for the greater good."

I waggled my eyebrows at her, hoping she'd start thinking about some Fred founding principle that gave us permission to tell white lies. I couldn't come up with any, but Zeba seemed like someone who'd paid a lot more attention to her Fred-parents and Fred-teachers than I had.

I just hoped she didn't think about the Fred founding principle that went, *For every good reason there is to lie, there is usually a better reason to tell the truth.*

Zeba cleared her throat.

"I didn't want to brag," she said. "But I am a pretty good basketball player."

I did a double take, and Zeba kept smiling. Whoa. Maybe she had just been planning to say, *Edwy, that's not something you would know, because you've never seen me play.* Maybe she really was a great basketball player. Maybe it was like how Rosi was better than me. Not just because she was taller—but because she was more coordinated, too.

Maybe Zeba was like that as well.

Oh, Rosi, you go missing and now I'm even willing to admit that you're better at most sports than I am. . . .

"Okay, then," I said out loud. "Zeba can borrow my basketball gear. Why don't you two get out of here so you're not late to the game? And so Kiandra can start helping me find Rosi?"

It seemed to take forever to dig out my orange basketball shirt for Zeba to wear, even though it was in a heap on top of my dresser. It seemed to take another forever for Enu and Zeba to leave. As soon as the door closed behind them, Kiandra leaned against it with a grin on her face.

"Okay, *that* was fun," she said.

"And now you're going to help me—" I began, tugging on Kiandra's arm, tugging her toward the kitchen table, where she'd put down her laptop.

But she shook me off.

"What? You believed me?" she asked. "No—I was just messing with Enu. I'm going back to bed. *That's* what I'm doing today."

She stepped past me, like it wouldn't even matter if I protested. Maybe she didn't expect me to protest. Maybe the whole time I'd been living with her and Enu, she'd gotten the impression that I could be easily brushed aside. That I could be distracted with basketball and video games.

That *was* how I'd been acting for the past week and a half.

As far as she knew, I'd just gone back to bed and fallen right to sleep last night.

I remembered what I'd yelled at her in the middle of the night: *Nobody gave me a choice going to Fredtown! Nobody gave me a choice going to Cursed Town! Nobody gave me a choice coming here!*

But I faced a choice now. I could let Kiandra walk right past me, and I could act like a typical Ref City kid, too cool to get upset about much of anything.

Or I could try everything I could to get Kiandra to help me. I couldn't be sure that she *would* help me. But I could make sure that *I* tried my hardest.

I grabbed Kiandra's arm again, and this time I didn't let go.

"You *have* to help me," I said. "Because I won't leave you alone until you do. I'll be the most annoying kid brother ever. I won't let you sleep. I won't let you eat. I'll just stand around forever saying, 'Find Rosi. Find Rosi. Help me find Rosi. . . .' You think girls are so important? She's a girl! And she needs a lot more help than getting into a basketball game!"

Kiandra blinked sleepily at me and looked down at my hand on her arm. She rubbed her eyes.

"Who's this Rosi again?" she asked.

CHAPTER
TWENTY-FOUR

Rosi didn't exist.

At first that was what it seemed like, from everything Kiandra found online. The Rosi Alvaran who showed up in the official records seemed to be a hardened criminal, a constant troublemaker. A rabble-rouser.

That wasn't at all the Rosi that I knew.

In the official records, it looked like Rosi had purposely started a battle in Cursed Town, then arranged for her coconspirators to smuggle her out of prison.

"This girl is amazing!" Kiandra kept saying, flipping through official-looking websites. "There's a reward for her capture? And it doesn't matter if she's caught dead or alive?"

That word, "dead," stabbed at me, and for a moment I couldn't even breathe, let alone answer Kiandra.

"And look—there's commentary about her from all over the planet," Kiandra went on. "All over the galaxy, really. She's famous! Or infamous—which is even cooler. What was she trying to do when she started everyone fighting in that marketplace? Did being raised in Fredtown make her hate humans? Was she secretly an alien trying to get humans to violate the rules, so Enforcers would have to invade?"

"Rosi didn't hate anyone," I insisted. "She'd never want people to fight. And she *wasn't* an alien. She *isn't*."

"Kiddo, until last night you didn't even know that the people who *raised* you were aliens," Kiandra said, glancing up from her laptop long enough to frown at me. "Excuse me for not trusting your opinion."

"I know what I'm talking about!" I said. "I always knew there was *something* wrong with the Freds. I just didn't know what it was. There was never anything wrong with Rosi."

My vision blurred, a problem I'd been having constantly since Kiandra had started helping me. I blinked hard.

"I don't care what other people are saying about Rosi," I told Kiandra. "I just want to know where she is. And if she's okay."

Kiandra narrowed her eyes at me, thought for a moment, and went back to typing.

"Aha!" she said. "I thought I could find a translation app for this. . . . Could it really be that I know how to do something that no news agency in the entire galaxy has figured out?"

"Translation app?" I repeated. "What are you talking about?"

"There's no audio with that videotape of your friend Rosi in the marketplace," Kiandra explained. "But I know an app that's pretty good at reading lips in videos without sound. . . . Yeah, here it is."

She turned the laptop toward me so I could see the screen too. It showed the scene of the Cursed Town marketplace again. Kiandra had frozen the video at the exact moment when Rosi, with Bobo on her back, climbed up onto the table. As soon as Rosi began to shout, I heard a robotic voice call out, "Everybody! Listen!"

"That's not how Rosi sounds," I objected.

"I didn't say this app reproduces her exact voice," Kiandra said. "It isn't scanning her vocal cords. But it can tell her exact words."

She rewound the video, starting over. Rosi appeared to scramble down and then back up onto the table in the Cursed Town marketplace.

"Everybody! Listen!" the robotic voice said again, perfectly matched to the movement of Rosi's lips. This time Kiandra let the video keep playing, with the robot voice continuing to speak Rosi's words. "A boy has gone missing. Maybe he's even been kidnapped. It's Edwy Watanaboneset. He's twelve, the same age as me. Please help. Please, we've got to organize a search. . . ."

Kiandra stopped the video. Rosi stayed frozen on the

screen, a man's fist mere centimeters away from punching into her stomach.

"This girl risked getting beat up just because she was worried about *you*?" Kiandra asked. "Because she wanted to rescue *you*?"

CHAPTER TWENTY-FIVE

"I . . . I guess so," I told Kiandra, as soon as I could trust my voice. It still came out husky and vulnerable. I tried to cover by imitating some of Enu's swagger. "What can I say? People love me."

To my surprise Kiandra threw out an arm that caught me right in the shoulder and knocked me back against the couch.

"Do *not* be like that," she commanded. "Your friend here is in serious trouble, and it looks like it was all because she cared about *you*."

That was exactly what I'd been trying to avoid thinking.

Kiandra stabbed her finger on the laptop keyboard, and the video advanced: the fist landing in Rosi's stomach, her pitching forward, hands grabbing her and throwing her to the ground.

I couldn't watch.

"But that doesn't make sense!" I insisted. "Why is this

my fault? I'm sorry I couldn't get word to Rosi that I wasn't exactly in any danger when Udans kidnapped me—or let her know that I'm perfectly safe here in Ref City. But when Rosi was in that marketplace, it's not like she was telling people, 'Hey! Let's go to war! Let's fight a battle because of Edwy!' She was just asking for help!"

"How long did you spend in Cursed Town?" Kiandra asked, as if I'd said something incredibly stupid.

"Like, barely a *day*," I protested.

"Yeah? Well, five minutes should have been enough for you to see that those people are seriously messed up," Kiandra said. "Couldn't you tell that people hate our family, because our father has so much power? Just saying our last name—Watanaboneset—it's like that Rosi girl was asking to get beat up!"

I remembered how Rosi's parents in Cursed Town had looked at me, the one time they'd met me. Rosi's brother, Bobo, had told them my last name, and Rosi's dad had muttered, *That pack of thieves.*

At the time I'd thought, *Hey, that's kind of cool! My family is notorious! Rosi's parents are afraid of me!*

But maybe this was the answer to what I'd wondered back in Cursed Town: how my dad could get away with stealing other people's possessions. Maybe he didn't get away with it, not really. Maybe it seemed like he did, because he never had to give anything back—maybe he always had so much power that people were too scared to go up to him and say, *Hey! That's mine! You can't take things that actually belong to me!* But that didn't mean that there weren't any. . .

Consequences, I told myself, landing on the one word that the Freds had probably said to me the most, every single time I misbehaved in Fredtown.

There had been consequences for my father stealing other people's possessions. And one of those consequences had been Rosi getting punched in the stomach.

"Yeah, okay, I can see why people might hate our mom and dad," I admitted to Kiandra.

"It's not just our mom and dad," Kiandra muttered. "It's everyone related to them, even distantly. Remember that awful story our father told about our ancestors, our 'noble tribe' of mighty men? About how we're better than other people, because we have green eyes? It was stories like that— attitudes like that—that made people hate us. That made—"

I was not going to sit there listening to her talk about ancient history.

"Okay, okay." I stopped Kiandra, shoving her away. "I get it. People have hated our family—our tribe—for generations. But why is it a crime for Rosi just to say my name? Why would anyone blame her? Why would they arrest *her,* after other people beat her up? When I was in Cursed Town, it didn't even seem like they had a police force, let alone a prison!"

I didn't think I had to say, *Or else wouldn't our own father have been sent to prison for stealing things that didn't belong to him?*

Kiandra clicked through screenfuls of information.

"I don't think there ever was much of a police force in Cursed Town," she said. "Nobody really enforced any laws. Except, you know, our dad making sure nobody stole anything back from *him*. He enforced his own rules, and that was as much law as there was. It's not like Ref City, where people know that if they step out of line, they'll get kicked out."

"Kicked out?" I repeated. "Don't people have a right to a fair trial? Aren't there judges and juries and elected officials who—"

Kiandra snorted, and I saw how much I sounded like a Fred.

"Sure, and everyone skips through daisies on the way to city council meetings," she said. She bumped her shoulder mockingly against mine. "I guess when the United Nations started Ref City, the plan was to work toward democracy and self-rule. Ref City *is* a lot better than Cursed Town. But, see, things are different now, all over the planet. All of humanity had to agree to follow a bunch of new rules, in order to get you and the other little kids back from the Freds."

I thought about objecting to Kiandra calling me a little kid. But I wanted to hear what she was going to say next.

"And one of those rules," she said, "was that if fighting broke out in any community, these really nasty aliens called Enforcers could come in and stop the fighting. After the fighting in Cursed Town, the Enforcers came in. And now they're allowed to stay forever. They're allowed to do anything they want to keep the peace." She looked me up and down. "I don't think it was a good trade."

Ouch.

"Again—not my fault!" I complained. "And not Rosi's fault either! Why . . . why wasn't there sound with the video of the Cursed Town marketplace to begin with? No offense, but how is it that nobody but you figured out a way to read Rosi's lips? If the police—or whoever, those Enforcers—if they'd heard what Rosi actually said, I bet she *wouldn't* have been arrested for fighting!"

"Yeah . . . you're probably right," Kiandra agreed, almost absentmindedly. She was scanning the screen again. "At least, she shouldn't have been arrested. I think it was kind of a setup. Maybe these Enforcers provided the video. Maybe they're the ones who wanted to make it look like more of a battle than it really was. Except . . ." She slumped back against the couch. "People really did fight in Cursed Town.

Your friend really did break a rule by escaping from prison."

"So we can't ever find her," I muttered, slumping in defeat. "If those Enforcer types haven't found her, we won't be able to either."

"Oh, I didn't say that," Kiandra said, still peering at the screen. She typed long strings of information. "What do you know? Looks like I can hack into alien computer systems too!" She turned the screen toward me. "Want to look at the people who were interrogated about Rosi's disappearance? Maybe we can figure out some clues the aliens couldn't see!"

CHAPTER
TWENTY-SIX

A man appeared on the screen, sitting at a table in front of a boring gray wall. The words WITNESS/POSSIBLE ACCESSORY #1, CASE #1 were stamped below his image.

"Is this anyone you know?" Kiandra asked.

"Rosi's dad," I said. "Her real . . . er, her father in Cursed Town."

Strangely, I could refer to my own parents as "real," and I'd slipped into thinking that way about Zeba's dad at the Ref City soup kitchen. But it seemed like for Rosi, her Fred-parents were the ones who deserved the name "real parents," more than the parents who'd given birth to her. Was it just because Rosi was so much more *like* her Fred-parents?

I didn't think Kiandra could help me figure that out.

"Rosi's dad—really?" she asked. "He's kind of scary-looking, isn't he? He must have lost his arm in the war."

I looked again. When I'd met Rosi's parents in Cursed Town, I hadn't paid any more attention to them than I usually paid to adults. That is to say: I'd lied to them, and I'd kind of gloated that they probably knew I was lying but couldn't prove it.

I hadn't known about the war back then. I'd barely noticed that Rosi's father was missing an arm. And that wasn't what made him scary, anyhow. It was the deep lines carved into his face. It was the anger that seemed entrenched in his very skin, as if he'd been mad for years, maybe for decades—for so long that his whole face had become a mask of fury.

He *was* scary-looking.

But something made me defend him.

"You don't like people judging you on how *you* look, Kiandra," I said accusingly. "Do you think it's his fault, what he looks like?"

"Touché," Kiandra mumbled. She reached for the keyboard. "Let's hear what he told the Enforcers."

On the screen Rosi's dad raised his head. Someone we couldn't see asked, "Where is your daughter?"

"I doan know," Rosi's father groaned. "Doan you thunk I'd tell you if'n I did?"

"That's not how he talked before!" I said. "It's like he's making himself sound stupider than he really is!"

Kiandra raised an eyebrow.

"That's kind of smart," she said admiringly.

"We know your daughter was present in your home after

she escaped from prison," the interrogator said, still offscreen. "Our patroller called it in . . . before he vanished. You have a lot to answer for, Nelsi Alvaran."

Rosi's dad reached across his body and held up his empty shirtsleeve.

"You think I coulda done anything to an Enforcer?" he asked. "Or even captured my own daughter? Me, one-armed and blind?"

"He's blind, too?" Kiandra said, and even she sounded distressed by this news.

"Could you just tell us what happened that night?" the interrogator asked. *He* didn't sound like he cared about Rosi's father's problems.

"Oh, be careful," I whispered. I knew from all the times I'd gotten caught lying in Fredtown: It's the open-ended questions that can trip you up.

Rosi's father nodded once and squinted his milky eyes.

"I's sitting in my own home, minding my own business," he said. "The girl show up and say she's goin' steal our boy from us. Our boy! The one we really care about!"

"Sexist, awful . . ." Kiandra muttered.

"Don't you think he could be pretending about that, too?" I asked Kiandra.

She didn't answer.

"Go on," the interrogator prompted.

"Minute later, patroller break down our door, screaming 'bout the girl," Rosi's father continued. "Girl shove past me, trying to get away. She knock me over. Clean over! I hit my head and black out. Wake up to you sticking da gun in my face and screaming questions."

Kiandra froze the action on the screen and turned to me.

"Do you think he's telling the truth?" she asked. "You know the man."

"I met him once for five minutes!" I protested. I didn't admit that Rosi had told me about her father too. Something about how he didn't like her nose. It hadn't made sense to me at the time—all I'd really noticed was how sad it made Rosi.

I focused on Kiandra's question.

"It *is* really convenient that Rosi's dad blacked out and couldn't capture Rosi and give her back to the Enforcers," I said. "And that would also mean he didn't know what happened to the patroller. But saying that is kind of a risky strategy if it isn't true."

I liked talking about this as if I were just evaluating lying skills. Not looking for clues that could save Rosi's life.

Kiandra restarted the video.

"You expect me to believe that you were unconscious until *I* showed up?" the interrogator roared at Rosi's father. "So of course you couldn't see what happened to the girl, you couldn't see what happened to our patroller, you couldn't see—"

"I couldn't *see* nothing nohow," Rosi's father interrupted. "Haven't seen nothing in twelve years. Can't never be no eyewitness for you."

His face was still scary, and he still wasn't talking right. And he was saying he couldn't see. But there was something strangely powerful in how Rosi's father answered that question, something that reminded me of my own father, even though the two men looked nothing alike.

Rosi's father seemed almost dignified.

The scene on the laptop screen dissolved into static and fuzz, and I jumped at the louder noise.

"I hope that was the end of that interrogation," Kiandra whispered. "I hope they didn't . . . hurt him."

"Hurt him?" I repeated. "What are you talking about? He answered the question!"

"Oh, Edwy, there's so much you don't know about how the universe works," Kiandra said, as if I were a preschooler. Maybe even a toddler.

I would have protested, but Kiandra was already summoning up the next interrogation. The words WITNESS/ POSSIBLE ACCESSORY #2, CASE #1 appeared at the bottom of the screen before the scene focused in.

This time, a woman sat at the same interrogation table, in front of the same blank gray wall.

"Rosi's mother," I told Kiandra, and Kiandra winced.

"Her face," she said. "Was it burned in the war? And then she probably didn't get good treatment, so it didn't heal right. . . ."

"How am I supposed to know?" I asked. "Remember, I'm the one who doesn't know how the universe works!"

"Just see if you can figure out anything from what she says," Kiandra muttered.

We both leaned back against the couch. Kiandra tilted the laptop so I could see the screen too. Rosi's mother had just started to protest, "I already told you everything I know. Poor women like me, it's not like we know much of anything!"

"You were there that night." It sounded like the same interrogator who'd questioned Rosi's father. "And surely *you're* not going to claim that you were unconscious too?"

"No, sir," Rosi's mother said. Her eyes darted to the side, which made her look sneaky.

No, no, I wanted to advise her. *When you're about to tell a lie, just keep looking straight ahead! Don't give yourself away!*

On the screen Rosi's mother straightened her back.

"I was there, but that don't mean I know anything," she said. "Girl came in and grabbed our boy; patroller came in and screamed at her; everyone ran away."

"And you were totally innocent," the interrogator said sarcastically.

"Yes, sir," Rosi's mother said. "Nothing I could do about any of it. You gonna pay to fix our front door? The one the patroller broke?"

"You were harboring a criminal!" the interrogator yelled. "Of course we're not going to pay to fix your door!"

"Girl ran through our house," Rosi's mother said with a shrug. "*Your* patroller chased her. Don't see how that's our fault."

"The pattern of footsteps in the mud around your house does *not* support your story," the interrogator growled.

"What footprints?" Rosi's mother asked. It seemed like she was trying to make her eyes look wide and innocent. But that didn't work very well with her scarred, haggard face.

I could almost hear the smile in the interrogator's voice.

"Exactly," he said. "Strangely enough, it looks as though someone tried to smooth away all evidence of footprints around your house."

Rosi's mother shrugged.

"It was nighttime, and I was wearing my robe," she said. "It's long. When I stepped outside to see where the girl and your patroller went, it musta drug on the ground."

Now the interrogator leaned toward her. I could see the back of his head: dark, matted hair.

"And yet, despite the attempt to destroy evidence, we were still able to make out some footprints," the interrogator purred. "Some *incriminating* footprints."

I was pretty sure Rosi's mother had been lying. But maybe she was better at it than me. She didn't even flinch.

"I don't know big words like that," she said.

"So many footprints were swept away," the interrogator said. "But it's clear there was a second woman at your house that evening. Maybe an accomplice?"

"Don't know that word neither," Rosi's mother said calmly. "We have neighbors stop by all the time. May have been someone there that afternoon. May have been someone there even earlier in the day. I don't keep track."

"I *might* have tried to work out a deal with you, if you'd confessed," the interrogator said. "If you'd told me the accomplice's name right away."

"You think I'm going to buy my own freedom, selling someone else's?" Rosi's mother asked. "You think I'm that lowdown?"

"Doesn't matter," the interrogator said. His back was still within the camera's range, and I saw his shoulders rise and fall in a cruel shrug. "Our patroller did an identity scan on your whole house, when he first got there. He sent that in even though, oddly, it was his last transmission. We *know* who else was in your house when the patroller arrived."

"If you already knew, why'd you bother asking me?" Rosi's mother said.

I wanted to tell Kiandra, *This isn't how Rosi's mother acted the last time I saw her*. The one time I'd seen the woman, she'd seemed mousy and angry and afraid. What had happened to turn her so brave, to give her the courage to talk back to an Enforcer?

But before I could say anything, a door opened near the table where Rosi's mother sat, and someone shoved a woman in a hooded cape into the interrogation room. She jolted against the table, almost falling, and the hood slipped from her hair.

"Oh no," I said. "Oh no."

"Do you know that woman?" Kiandra asked.

"She's a maid," I said.

"Why would that matter?" Kiandra began. "Unless—"

"She works for our parents," I said.

CHAPTER TWENTY-SEVEN

Kiandra grabbed my arm.

"Does this maid know anything about you?" she asked. "Anything about Enu and me?"

I shook Kiandra's hand away.

"Kiandra—I lived in our parents' house for barely twenty-four hours!" I protested. "I'm doing well to recognize her! To know anything!"

This wasn't entirely true. According to the Freds, one of my worst traits was that I liked to snoop in other people's things. I wasn't like my father—I never *stole* anything from anyone. But sometimes I just wondered what people kept in their cabinets and drawers, what they hid away and thought no one else needed to see.

If the Freds back in Fredtown had just been honest about everything from the start, I wouldn't have felt like I needed to be so sneaky, I thought, as if I needed to defend my motives.

But I didn't know that for sure. Maybe I would have been a curious kid no matter where I grew up.

Anyhow, just in the first night I'd spent in my parents' home, I'd wandered the whole house. I'd pulled out every drawer in my father's desk and looked at every piece of paper. I *hadn't* discovered any secret door down to the hidden tunnel and warehouse and office under my parents' house, but I'm sure I would have eventually.

On the screen Rosi's mother gasped.

"Drusa," she whispered, to my parents' maid. "Believe me, I didn't tell them about you. I didn't try to drag you into this. . . ."

The maid—Drusa?—hugged the other woman's shoulders.

"And I won't say anything about your daughter," she said. "I promise." She peered straight at the interrogator, which made it seem as though she was peering straight out at Kiandra and me. "Not that I know anything *to* say."

"Oh, how very sweet," the interrogator mocked them. "Of course neither of you knows anything. Let's see what you say *separately.*"

Guards came in and pulled Rosi's mother away. The interrogator ordered Drusa to sit in the abandoned chair. In the spotlight.

A new label appeared on the screen: WITNESS/POSSIBLE ACCESSORY #3, CASE #1.

"At least this woman looks normal," Kiandra muttered. "I bet she's a lot younger than Rosi's parents. And—she's a lot prettier."

Drusa's green eyes sparkled, while Rosi's mother's had been shadowed and scary. Freed from the hood, Drusa's long hair fell in waves down her back.

"Right, because what she looks like really matters right now," I told Kiandra.

Kiandra bit her lip.

"I guess it's a habit, always noticing what people look like," she said. "But in this case . . . maybe if the interrogator thinks she's pretty, she can sweet-talk him, and then—"

"What?" I said, a little too sharply. "Can she convince the Enforcers not to chase after Rosi? Not to even try to find her? Can she get them to stop saying they want Rosi captured, dead or alive?"

"Never mind," Kiandra whispered.

Drusa settled into the chair slowly, as if she wanted to make the interrogator wait.

"Can Mrs. Alvaran hear what I tell you?" Drusa asked. "Will either of the Alvarans know what I say here?"

"Of course not," the interrogator said. "What you say here is only between you and me."

"And all the rest of the Enforcers," Kiandra muttered. "And . . . anyone like me who can hack into their account."

But Drusa was nodding trustingly at the interrogator.

"That's good," she said, leaning forward. "Because I think I can help you find the outlaw."

CHAPTER TWENTY-EIGHT

"**Why, that dirty,** double-crossing . . . *snake*!" Kiandra exclaimed, jolting back so dramatically that the laptop almost fell to the floor. I had to grab it and hold it steady.

"Shh, shh, let's hear what she has to say," I begged Kiandra. "Maybe whatever she tells the interrogator, that will make it so *we* can find Rosi first. . . ."

"Edwy, this interrogation took place a week and a half ago," Kiandra reminded me, but I ignored her. I turned up the volume on the laptop, so I could hear the conversation between Drusa and the interrogator better.

"Now, why would you help us?" the interrogator asked. "Why would you betray your neighbors—and your entire species?"

"Because I know your people are in charge now," Drusa said. "Because, what are my neighbors to me anyway? And because—did you know that that evil child Rosi stole *my* daughter when she ran away?"

"Rosi would never do that!" I protested, and now it was Kiandra's turn to shush me.

The interrogator leaned across the table. I still couldn't see anything but the back of his head and now the top part of his dark uniform, but I could tell from his voice that he was smiling again.

"Please explain," he purred. "Our theory was that *you* had perhaps sent your child away with Rosi and her brother Bobo, because you misguidedly thought that was a route to safety, rather than a path to death. And I assure you: Your daughter *will* die. She will die a horrible death unless you come clean and help us find how to rescue her. How many more deaths are necessary—two? Or three?"

"That's, that's—" I gasped.

"Blackmail," Kiandra muttered beside me. "Emotional manipulation."

Drusa winced, but she also leaned closer to the interrogator.

"It would not be fair for you to punish my daughter for the other girl's crimes!" she protested. "Not when my daughter was taken as a hostage . . ."

The interrogator recoiled.

"A hostage?" he said, surprise in his tone. He looked down, as if peering at notes on the table in front of him. "Your daughter Cana is five, correct?"

"Drusa is *Cana's* mother?" I asked. "That's who she's talking about?"

"You know this Cana?" Kiandra asked.

"Of course," I said. "Back in Fredtown, everybody knew everybody. It wasn't like Ref City, where people just pass each other on the street. Or Cursed Town, where . . ."

"Where people fight," Kiandra finished for me.

I had to look away. I let myself think about Fredtown, about all the community events there: the endless school programs and the potluck suppers and the group birthday parties that occurred once a month, celebrating everybody born in March, everyone born in April, and so on. I'd probably started whining, *Do I have to go?* to my Fred-parents way back when I was a toddler. I hated all those community events. But now . . .

Was it possible that I missed even that aspect of Fredtown now?

I squeezed my eyes shut, then opened them again.

"Cana was the smartest of all the little kids in Fredtown," I told Kiandra. "Sometimes she figured out things I couldn't."

Things . . . and people, I thought.

Cana had been the one who'd told me Rosi was just as upset as I was about going back to our real parents and their hometown—to Cursed Town. Because all I'd seen was Rosi doing what the Freds wanted her to. Just like she always did.

But Cana had brushed her little curls out of her face and whispered, *No, Rosi's sad and worried. She just doesn't want anyone to see her cry. . . .*

"Maybe it's genetic," Kiandra said, and I had to snap my attention back to remembering she was talking about Cana, not Rosi. "Maybe her mother's really smart too, and she knows exactly what she's doing, playing out some story for the interrogator."

"Yes, my daughter Cana is five," Drusa was telling the interrogator. "So?"

"You expect me to believe that humans are such vile creatures that a twelve-year-old girl would take a five-year-old girl hostage?" the interrogator asked.

Drusa lowered her head and narrowed her eyes at him.

"You are sitting in Cursed Town, the scene of a massacre so horrible that twelve years ago alien creatures had to intervene to stop it," Drusa said. "And now *you* are here to stop the warfare that started today. And you have to ask if humans are vile creatures?"

"Whose side is she on?" Kiandra asked.

"There were rumors flying that the Alvaran girl had escaped from prison," Drusa said. "I went to their house to warn her parents that they couldn't expect any help from anyone in the neighborhood if they tried to hide her. But when I stepped through the frot door, the girl was already there. The patroller arrived a moment later, and when he tried to capture the girl, she grabbed my daughter Cana and held her body like a shield, to keep the patroller from attacking."

"That would be . . . against our protocol," the interrogator said.

"Wait—does he mean it would be against their protocol to attack someone with a five-year-old hostage, or against their protocol to care?" Kiandra asked.

I didn't know, so I didn't answer.

Drusa let out a sob.

"Please find my little girl," she said. "Please bring her back to me."

"You have to help us," the interrogator said. "Tell us everything you know about this Rosi. Even if you never met her except when she kidnapped your daughter, you must have heard lots of rumors about her in your town."

"Oh, but I did meet her before tonight!" Drusa said, reaching across the table as if she were about to grab the interrogator's hand. Then she stopped herself, as if it would have been too presumptuous to touch the interrogator. "Rosi and her brother, Bobo, came to the Watanabonesets', where I work, earlier today. This afternoon. Right before the riot in the marketplace."

"Indeed?" the interrogator asked, a certain slyness back in his voice. "Please, tell me what happened."

"Edwy, is this true?" Kiandra whispered. "Was Rosi at our parents' house?"

"How would I know?" I said helplessly. "Drusa's talking about what happened on Monday afternoon. I was already in the truck with Udans then, on my way to Ref City."

I watched the gleam in Drusa's eyes, the animated way she waved her hands, telling her story.

"Rosi knocked at the door, asking if her friend Edwy could come out and play," Drusa said. "But Edwy was already out playing—wandering the town, most likely, up to no good. You know how boys that age are."

Even if Drusa didn't know Rosi very well, it seemed like she'd figured me out. Well enough to have come up with a plausible-sounding lie about where I'd been that afternoon.

"So then this Rosi left?" the interrogator asked.

"I *thought* so," Drusa said. "But a few minutes later, I discovered she'd sneaked into the Watanabonesets' house."

"Rosi would never do that!" I protested. "Not *Rosi*! That just isn't—"

"Shh," Kiandra said. "You made me miss the rest of what Drusa said."

She had to back up the video a little, so once again we heard Drusa say, ". . . sneaked into the Watanabonesets' house."

And then Drusa went on: "I found the girl in Mr. Watanaboneset's office. I chased her away."

"Did you tell your employers?"

Drusa shook her head.

"I was afraid they'd fire me, if they thought the girl had gotten in because I forgot to latch the door."

"That *is* plausible," Kiandra mumbled. "Our parents would fire a maid without even thinking about it."

"So nothing really came of your encounter with Rosi, earlier in the day," the interrogator said. "You've wasted our time, telling me this story."

"No, no—you haven't let me finish!" Drusa said. "Later, after I heard what that girl did in the marketplace, I went back to my employer's office. I started worrying . . . what if she'd stolen something? What if, when I chased her away, she'd already taken something that was small enough to hide in her clothing?"

"And did she?" the interrogator asked, leaning so far forward now that he practically could have kissed Drusa's cheek. "Was anything like that missing from Mr. Watanaboneset's desk?"

"Yes, sir," Drusa said. "A map. Rosi stole a map."

I buried my face in my hands and moaned, "No . . ."

CHAPTER
TWENTY-NINE

"What's wrong with you?" Kiandra asked.

"I looked through everything in our father's desk!" I confessed. "There was only one map in there! It had one route marked on it. I know Rosi wouldn't steal a map, but . . . what if she saw it? And memorized it? Rosi's really good at memorizing stuff. If Drusa tells the interrogator about that map, the Enforcers will know right where to find Rosi!"

Kiandra tilted her head to look sideways at me.

"But didn't you just say Drusa was lying?" she asked. "If you think she was lying about Rosi taking this kid Cana hostage, why would you think she's telling the truth about some map?"

Oh yeah, lies, I thought.

It was weird—I'd been so used to telling lies myself, back in Fredtown. But I was also used to the Freds either telling the truth or giving some non-answer like *You'll learn that when you're older.* (I *hated* that reply!) The little kids I'd been around lied sometimes, but their lies were so obvious, it was easy to figure them out.

So as much as I'd lied, I didn't have much practice with figuring out if someone else was lying or telling the truth.

I'd watched Rosi's mom and dad and had been pretty sure they were lying. But Drusa seemed much better at it. So . . . I didn't know.

I looked back at the screen and realized Kiandra had frozen the action. She ran a finger back and forth on the keyboard, making the cursor jump around.

"What *was* the map you saw at our parents' house?" Kiandra asked. "Why is Drusa even bringing it up?"

"I don't know," I admitted. "It showed a river, and mountains, and—"

"Cursed Town? Refuge City?" Kiandra asked. She typed something quickly. "Was it one of these?"

She called up a whole array of maps depicting Cursed Town. Then she opened a new screen and opened a bunch of maps showing Refuge City.

"No," I said impatiently. "Don't you think I would have remembered the name if I'd seen the words 'Cursed Town' on that map? Or 'Refuge City'? Don't you think I would have asked someone about it?"

"Hmm," Kiandra said. "Then maybe . . ."

She began typing again. I saw the words "out-of-date" before a new screenful of maps opened up.

These maps showed creeks and rivers and mountains much more prominently. The only settlements listed seemed to be small towns and villages, with names like Loveliness and Joy and Beautiful View.

"Kind of the opposite of Cursed Town, huh?" I joked.

"These are bad translations of the language people used to speak around here before everyone agreed to one universal language," Kiandra said. "Don't look at the names. Look at the things that don't change, or that don't change for millennia at a time."

The mountains, the rivers . . . , I thought.

"Oh!" I jerked upright, and pointed at one of the first maps on the screen. "That tiny pinpoint beside the mountains—that's Refuge City, isn't it? And this town—Loveliness? Really?— that's where Cursed Town is today. I see it now, because of where the creek bends. Kiandra, *this* is the map our father had in his desk. Only there was a route drawn between Loveliness and the pinpoint that was going to become Refuge City. . . ."

"I thought so," Kiandra said triumphantly, as if she'd been the one to figure everything out. "Edwy, this is a copy of the map that Udans used to bring Enu and me here to Refuge City. It was how he found Refuge City, when it had just begun. When it was just refugees and aid workers here."

I stared at the map, trying to ignore the weird, overly hopeful names.

"It's missing something else," I said. "That thick dark line you said was the border . . ."

"That's because there wasn't a border when this map

was made," Kiandra said. "It's from before the war."

"Oh," I said.

Kiandra switched back to the scene she'd frozen of the interrogator and Drusa. She started the video again.

"What was on the map you say Rosi stole?" the interrogator asked. He bent forward, as if writing something down. I hadn't seen him write anything down when Rosi's parents were speaking.

"It showed a route out of Cursed Town," Drusa said. "South, along the creek . . ."

"She's awful!" I shouted. "Despicable. There's no way Rosi kidnapped Cana. So why does Drusa want to help the Enforcers catch Rosi?"

Kiandra flipped back to the old map showing Loveliness and just the beginnings of Refuge City.

"Edwy, look—south goes toward the bottom of the map; north, toward the top," Kiandra said, pointing. "Refuge City is north of Cursed Town. Drusa didn't tell the Enforcers which way Rosi went, if Rosi followed this map. Drusa told them to go the opposite way!"

I felt a glimmer of hope. But only a moment of staring at the map made the hope die.

"But would Rosi know about the border?" I asked. "If she's coming toward Refuge City, how's she going to cross the border?"

"How would she cross the border if she's trying to escape from Cursed Town in any direction?" Kiandra asked. "Nobody can cross the border!"

I stared at Kiandra, and she stared right back—grimly, without blinking. Kiandra was saying there was nothing we could do: Rosi, Bobo, and Cana were doomed to be caught.

She was saying Rosi, Bobo, and Cana were doomed to die.

I shoved the laptop away.

"You're wrong!" I said. I wasn't sure if I was arguing against Kiandra's words or just the hopeless tone in her voice. Her despair fit with everything else people kept saying to me in Refuge City, from Enu's *Why think about unpleasant things you can't do anything about?* to Kiandra's *Don't ask questions like that ever again* to Udans's *That's just how life goes* and *There's nothing you can do.*

Udans.

I jumped to my feet.

"Udans can cross the border!" I reminded Kiandra. I remembered that I'd been too timid to ask him about Rosi before. But that was before I knew Rosi was being hunted down. And before Kiandra had shown me maps and interrogations. "And you're going to help me figure out how to get him to rescue Rosi. Before she even *gets* to that border!"

CHAPTER
THIRTY

"Why would Udans help?" Kiandra asked.

"Because, because . . . it's the right thing to do!" I said.

I had never sounded so much like a Fred in my entire life. Kiandra snorted.

"Oh, right, because that's what Udans cares about," she muttered. "Sometimes, Edwy, I think those Freds really did turn you into an alien creature. Are we talking about the same Udans? All he cares about is obeying our father so our father doesn't fire him!"

"Then . . . we convince him our father wants him to rescue Rosi," I said. "We convince him he'll be fired if he *doesn't* rescue Rosi!"

"Don't you think Enu and I have tried a million times to convince Udans that our father would want Udans to just obey *us*?" she asked. "Udans may be a country bumpkin, but he's not stupid!"

"Kiandra, I have to try," I said. "I have to do everything I can for Rosi. When will Udans be back? How often does he come to visit?"

This wasn't like me, to state something so plainly. I wasn't joking, wasn't lying, wasn't being snarky or sarcastic. It was as if I'd ripped open my chest and was letting Kiandra watch my heart beat.

Kiandra ran her fingers back and forth over the keyboard. It reminded me of the way little kids back in Fredtown comforted themselves rubbing their hands or faces against a favorite blanket or stuffed animal.

"Udans may still be in Ref City," she said slowly, almost as if she was trying to make up her mind. I'd never heard Kiandra sound so indecisive. "He was just here yesterday afternoon, and he wouldn't have started back to Cursed Town so late in the day. He probably loaded up his truck last night, checked into some flea-bitten hotel, and planned to get back on the road first thing this morning."

I'd lost all track of time. It'd been early—practically still nighttime—when I'd gone to the soup kitchen and met Zeba. It had still been early when I'd gotten back to our apartment, and when Zeba had left with Enu for the basketball game. But how long had Kiandra and I spent watching Rosi's parents and Drusa being interrogated?

What would Udans count as "first thing in the morning"?

It was ridiculously optimistic of me—ridiculously

Fred-like—but I decided to believe that we still had time.

"Then let's go to his hotel right now!" I cried. "Before he leaves!"

"What makes you think I would know where Udans is staying?" Kiandra asked, still aimlessly running a finger over the keyboard.

"Because if you didn't, you'd say so," I told her.

Kiandra didn't say anything.

"Kiandra, I can't do this without you," I whispered. "Didn't you want to have a choice about something important? This is important! It's—it's life or death! This is your chance to make a bigger decision than how to paint your nails or what dress to wear!"

Kiandra winced. Then she straightened up, as if I'd said the magic words. Her fingers spun across the laptop keys, full of purpose now.

"Our father keeps a tracker on Udans," she said. "Udans thinks it's practically magic, the way our father always seems to know where Udans stops for lunch, where he encounters the worst traffic, and so on. But it's really because of me. Me tracking Udans online, and tattling to our father."

"What? I thought you hated our parents!" I asked, baffled. The more I got to know about Kiandra, the more she confused me.

"They're still our parents," Kiandra murmured.

A map of Refuge City came up on the laptop screen. A dot blinked at a crossroads in an unfamiliar part of the city. I realized it wasn't far from the soup kitchen where I'd met Zeba.

"Udans is still at the hotel," Kiandra said.

I grabbed her arm.

"Then let's go!"

Kiandra winced, and I realized I'd screamed a little too loudly in her ear.

"Let me just . . . grab my bag first," she muttered. "And we'll take the laptop with us, so we can keep tracking Udans. . . ."

It seemed to take forever for her to get ready. But finally we were out on the landing by the elevator.

"Hurry up, hurry up . . . ," I chanted, as if that could make the elevator come faster.

The elevator dinged, the doors opened—and there were Enu and Zeba, back from their basketball game.

"Kiandra?" Enu asked, as if she was the only one he noticed. He stepped into the doorway of the elevator, holding it open. "You're actually leaving the apartment?"

"I'm helping Edwy," Kiandra said, swaying slightly. "He thinks Udans might be able to rescue his friend."

Enu looked from Kiandra to me.

"So could you move out of the way?" I asked impatiently.

"We've got to get to Udans's hotel before he leaves!"

Enu glanced back at Zeba.

"I'll come too," he said.

"Could you use my help as well?" Zeba asked.

I pictured all four of us kids lined up in front of Udans. More people would be more convincing, wouldn't they?

"Sure," I said. "Thanks."

Enu moved back out of the way. Kiandra and I stepped into the elevator, and it zoomed down to the ground floor. Enu put his hand on Kiandra's elbow, guiding her out of the elevator, across the lobby, and out onto the street.

Finally, as she took a step into the sunshine, she shook Enu's hand away.

"Enu, I'll be fine," she insisted.

Enu just grabbed her other elbow.

"Just making sure . . . ," he muttered.

"Why wouldn't she be fine?" I asked, annoyed that they were slowing us down *again*.

Zeba watched Kiandra carefully.

"Is she sick?" Zeba asked.

"No!" Kiandra insisted.

"Yes!" Enu countered. "She never leaves our apartment!"

Kiandra stared back at him with great dignity.

"Maybe I just didn't have a reason to, until now," she said. "Did you ever think of that?"

CHAPTER
THIRTY-ONE

We found Udans beside his truck.

He was still in the parking lot behind his hotel, double-checking the lock on the back of his truck. He gasped when he saw Enu, Kiandra, and me.

"No," he said firmly. "Your parents would *not* want you in this part of the city. You must go home immediately."

"Not until you help us," I said.

Udans glanced around. The blacktop we stood on was crumbling, and weeds grew up through the cracks. The back of the hotel building was covered with graffiti. Somewhere, not that far away, we could hear a siren.

Udans jerked on the lever at the back of the truck. The door rolled open.

"We'll talk inside the truck," he said. "Where no one will see that you're here. Then I'll drive you back to your apartment."

Enu and Kiandra looked at each other and shrugged.

They followed Udans into the cargo area of the truck, with me right behind them. I turned around to give Zeba a hand up too.

"I don't know her," Udans said. "She can stay outside."

"You'd make a young girl wait outside, *alone*, in this neighborhood?" Kiandra asked. "Udans, I'm ashamed of you."

"She's trustworthy," I said.

Udans frowned but stood aside to let Zeba scramble up.

"Hurry it up," he said. "Your father doesn't like it when I'm late with his supplies from the city."

"You're not taking him much this time, are you, Udans?" Enu asked, glancing around.

It was true—the back of the truck was only half full of boxes and crates. That meant that the cover to the secret compartment below the floor, where I'd hidden, should have been in plain view. But even knowing it was there, I still had to squint and study the floor carefully just to make out the outlines of the cover. The cracks around it seemed barely more noticeable than any of the other cracks in the floorboards.

"Ever since the Enforcers took over Cursed Town, it's been tough to convince our suppliers in Ref City that they'll be paid," Udans said, even as he pulled the back door of the truck shut, hiding us from view. He hit a switch that turned on an overhead light, which made everyone look a little ghostly. "So *my* job is harder than ever. You might tell your father that. Put in a good word for me."

I saw my opening.

"We'll tell him you're the greatest person ever, if you help us," I said. "See, I have this friend back in Cursed Town who's in danger. Really, it's three friends—my friend Rosi, her brother Bobo, and another kid, Cana. I just need you to find them and smuggle them here to Ref City."

Udans gaped at me.

"You mean Rosi the escaped criminal?" he asked. "That Rosi?"

"She's not actually a criminal," I began.

Udans began shaking his head.

"You think I'd get involved with rescuing her?" he asked. Maybe it was a trick of the wavering light, but it seemed like he had started to tremble. "Don't you know what she did?"

"Yes—she asked people to help rescue *me*," I said. My voice came out sounding too emotional. I cleared my throat. "I owe her."

"Then that's a debt you'll never be able to pay," Udans said. He appealed to Kiandra and Enu. "The two of you need to talk some sense into this boy before the next time I come back to Ref City. *You* know no one can change anything in Cursed Town."

"We don't think Rosi is in Cursed Town anymore,"

Kiandra said. "We think she's on her way toward Ref City with the two little kids."

"But she doesn't know about the border," I added. "We think she might be following the same route you did, bringing Enu and Kiandra to the city all those years ago."

"Then they're all as good as dead," Udans said.

"You don't even sound sorry about that," Zeba protested.

Udans gazed at her with hard eyes.

"If I sat around feeling sorry about things I can't change—things I couldn't ever have changed—I'd have died of grief years ago," he said. "You have to make the best of things."

That last part sounded like something a Fred would say. But they would have made the phrase "make the best of things" sound optimistic and hopeful. Coming out of Udans's mouth, the words sounded more like giving up.

How could I get so confused about what Freds would think and what Udans would think?

I shook my head and cleared my throat.

"That's all we want—to make the best of things," I said, trying to sound decisive. "And that means you need to rescue Rosi."

"I won't," Udans said. "That would be like asking for certain death."

"It wasn't certain death smuggling *me* across the border," I said. "You survived that."

"That's because the Enforcers weren't in power then," Udans said. He reached back for the door, as if he thought the conversation was over.

"I bet you'd do it for money," Enu sneered. "What if Edwy here offered you money? What's your price?"

Was Enu trying to help me or not?

"You little snot," Udans said, pulling himself to his full height, his head practically scraping the ceiling. He and Enu stood nose to nose. The ugliness that had lain between them yesterday was back. "Do you know what *my* life was like when I was your age? Believe me, I didn't have any Daddy Deep Pockets sending me money. And you dare to imply that there's something wrong with me, because I want enough money to live on? Enough money to eat?"

"Can we just get back to talking about Rosi?" I asked. I glanced around frantically in the dim light. My gaze finally lit on a crowbar hanging on the wall. I pulled it down and began prying at the cover over the hidden compartment in the floor.

"Hey! Hey! Don't do that!" Udans said, reaching for the crowbar. "Certain secrets need to stay secret!"

It was too late. I already had the cover halfway up.

"See, all you have to do is hide Rosi and Bobo and Cana down there," I said. "Nothing will happen!"

I pulled the crowbar back, so Udans couldn't grab it.

Enu lifted the cover the rest of the way up.

"Sweet!" Enu cried. "What do you normally use that space for, Udans? What are you smuggling that our father doesn't know about?"

"Nothing!" Udans said. "I am an honest man! You see, that space is totally empty!"

He bent down, trying to shove the cover back over the hidden compartment. He sprawled so desperately across the floor, something fell out of his pocket.

Keys. It was a set of keys.

Kiandra laughed and scooped them up.

"Did you lose something, Udans?" she asked, dangling the keys from her fingertips. "What if I just handed these over to Edwy and let him go rescue his friend himself?"

"You—you cannot—" Udans sputtered.

Part of my brain—the Fred-trained part—was frozen in horror: *How can Kiandra taunt Udans like that? How can she be so mean?*

But there was another part of my brain, the part that had always resisted all my Fred training. That part of my brain was gloating along with Kiandra: *We have the truck keys! Udans will never help us! Why don't we just help ourselves?*

I glanced down, my eyes falling on the crowbar in my hands. Udans was scrambling to his feet, ready to lunge for Kiandra.

While he was off-balance, perched on one knee at the edge of the secret compartment, I shoved the crowbar against his shoulder. Udans fell over backward, into the compartment.

"Quick!" I yelled at Enu and Zeba.

I slid the cover back over the compartment, smashing Udans down. I jumped on top of the cover, and a second later Enu and Zeba joined me. Kiandra began sliding boxes over it. In no time at all, the secret compartment was hidden again. I had no doubt that Udans was screaming, down in the secret compartment, but we couldn't hear him.

Zeba took a shaky breath and slumped against the wall.

"What have we done?" she asked.

"What we had to," Kiandra told her. She held up the keys. "Who wants to drive?"

CHAPTER
THIRTY-TWO

"Is it okay to do a bad thing for a good reason?" Zeba whispered to me.

We were sitting in the cab of Udans's truck. Enu was behind the steering wheel, with Kiandra beside him, her head bent over her laptop. She was navigating, telling him the best route for getting out of Refuge City.

That left Zeba and me crammed against the passenger-side door, and Zeba whispering about right and wrong.

"I don't know about bad things and good reasons," I said. "I just know we have to rescue Rosi."

"But Udans . . . ," Zeba began.

"He'll survive," I said. "We'll let him out of the secret compartment after we rescue Rosi. Everything will be fine."

Zeba was quiet for a minute.

"My dad says that's how the Freds thought," she said. "The ends justified the means. They thought it was okay to steal all of us kids away from our parents, if that made us grow up as nicer people. So that humans weren't a danger to the universe. They thought it was worth the . . . the 'moral ambiguity.' My dad says that's what it's called, when there's not a clear right or wrong answer."

"Rescuing Rosi isn't like that," I said. "I know it's right. Everything about it is right."

"But . . ." Zeba leaned closer, so she could whisper directly into my ear. "Is that what your brother and sister think? Is that why they're doing this? Can you really count on them to do the right thing when we get to the border?"

I stole a sidelong glance at Enu and Kiandra. Kiandra was mumbling, "Right turn here, then get into the left lane . . ." Enu was waving at people on the sidewalk and calling out, "Yeah, that's right, look at me, you suckers! You have to walk, but I've got wheels!"

I peered out the window, and the bustle and noise of Refuge City was as overwhelming as ever. Even with the sun high in the sky now, the city's lights blazed brightly—as if the people of Refuge City thought they could outshine the sun.

This is where I belong, I told myself, trying out the sentence in my head as if I still didn't believe it. *This is where I belong because* . . .

Because with all the lights and noise and bustle, you didn't have to listen to the thoughts in your own head. Unless there was some girl beside you who kept asking questions about right and wrong.

It wasn't just her question about what we'd done to Udans that bothered me. There was something else, too.

I sighed.

"Zeba, you don't have to come with us," I told her. "This might be dangerous. You don't even know Rosi. It's not your responsibility to help her."

"It *is* my responsibility to help her," Zeba countered. "It's my responsibility to help you. That's something I do know."

"Just because you were raised by Freds to do the right thing?" I asked. "Just because your parents here on Earth are the type of people who run a soup kitchen? Zeba, you are doubly doomed to be a do-gooder!"

"Don't you think I ever make my own decisions?" she asked fiercely.

"Do you?"

"Um . . . I don't know," Zeba said. She flashed me a trembling smile. "I'm trying to."

Beside me Kiandra chanted, "Left lane, left lane . . ."

Enu zoomed past an oncoming car and onto a highway.

"Did you see those mad skills?" he congratulated himself. "Oh man, this is so much better than driving in a video game!"

"So . . . have you ever driven a *real* car or truck before?"

Zeba asked. "Should I have asked that *before* I got into this truck with you?"

"Doesn't matter," Enu crowed. "Look how good I am at this! Who says video games don't teach you anything?"

He swerved around a slower-moving car.

"You do realize, if you crash, we could die for real, don't you?" Zeba asked.

"Killjoy," Enu muttered. "How about you just go back to looking pretty?"

"Enu!" Kiandra exploded. She started to elbow him, then seemed to remember that that could lead to him swerving once again.

"Kidding, kidding," Enu said. "Edwy, you were right. Your friend Zeba isn't *just* pretty. She's also an *awesome* basketball player. We've got hours before we'll get to the border. Zeba, how about we tell Kiandra and Edwy the play-by-play of how the game went?"

"I think I'll focus on researching everything I can about the border," Kiandra said.

"Good idea," I agreed. I leaned over so I could see her laptop screen too.

"Edwy, you're making it so I can barely breathe," Kiandra complained. "How about I just read anything interesting out loud?"

But I'd already caught a glimpse of an awful paragraph:

Since arriving on Earth, the Enforcers have made the border around Cursed Town the most impenetrable barrier in the universe. The Enforcers' new bioscans make it impossible to smuggle any life-form across the border. Their sensors can detect the presence of even the tiniest microbe.

I pointed at the laptop screen.

"Kiandra, how are we going to get around that?" I asked, my panic welling up.

She shoved her elbow into my ribs. It was almost as if I'd gotten the dig she'd wanted to give Enu.

"Edwy, do you really believe everything you read?" she asked. "*This* is what the Enforcers are telling *humans*. I need to see what the Enforcers are telling each other."

Her fingers flew over the laptop keys. I was careful not to crowd her, but I could see flashes of words: *Accident report . . . Malfunction report . . . Engineering update . . .*

She leaned her head back and practically cackled.

"You're *so* lucky you've got a brilliant sister," she told me. "I've got the perfect plan!"

Zeba caught my eye and raised an eyebrow, as if to say, *Is it the perfect plan for rescuing Rosi? Or is it just the perfect plan for Kiandra to show how brilliant she is?*

CHAPTER
THIRTY-THREE

We stopped a few kilometers back from the border to let Udans out of the secret compartment.

This was a compromise Zeba had urged on us.

"Having Udans in the truck won't help us unless he's the one handing his travel papers over to the border guard," she said. "And since he won't do that—and we're not even going through an official border crossing—all we're doing is putting his life in danger."

"He deserves to have his life in danger if he won't help us!" Enu muttered.

"Udans isn't your puppet," Zeba said. "Udans has a right to make his own decisions."

"Is this what it was like all the time, living in Fredtown?" Enu asked me. "People always telling you what they thought was the right thing to do? Without any sense of humor at all?"

"Yes!" I told him.

"I don't know how you survived it," Enu muttered.

Maybe I truly was his mini-me.

But Enu was the one who stopped the truck behind a towering rock formation. He was the one who found a rope. So when Zeba pried the cover off the secret compartment and Udans sprang out, Enu and I tackled him, and Kiandra tied the rope around Udans's wrists and ankles.

I couldn't have done this by myself, I thought. *I really did need Enu's and Kiandra's and Zeba's help.*

"You will regret this!" Udans screamed. "Listen to me— don't do this crazy thing! Let me drive you back to Refuge City where you'll be safe! None of you understand what the world's like—you've *all* been too sheltered! If you do this, you'll die!"

Zeba shivered at that, but Enu just said, "Kiandra, can you find a cloth so we can gag his mouth, too? So he'll shut up?"

Kiandra ripped off the bottom of her shirt and tied it around Udans's mouth. But he still grunted and squirmed and tried to kick as all four of us kids eased him down from the truck.

"Think about how strong you seemed, when it was you kidnapping me," I said to Udans. "Now that it's you against four of us, you're not so strong, are you?"

"Is this really about revenge?" Zeba asked me quietly.

"No, no . . . ," I muttered.

We half carried, half dragged Udans over to a signpost that pointed the way to Refuge City. Enu tied the ends of the rope to that signpost.

"This way, even if we don't make it back for you, someone will see you and rescue you," Zeba said. "*You'll* be safe, no matter what."

"Zeba, we're all going to be safe," Kiandra said confidently. "I've got the perfect plan, remember?"

"The Freds thought they did too," Zeba murmured, and Kiandra glared at her.

"We'll be back soon," I assured Udans. "Never fear."

Udans was still squirming and struggling when we drove away. I watched him in the rearview mirror until his tan clothes and brown face blended in with the tan and brown of the drought-stricken landscape around us.

Rosi, Bobo, and Cana have been out in the wilderness for a week and a half, I thought. *What if the greatest danger to them wasn't Enforcers, but . . . thirst and starvation? What if they're already dead and this is all for nothing?*

Maybe Enu and Zeba were thinking similar thoughts, because they both fell silent as we approached the border. Kiandra lowered her head closer and closer to her laptop, as if that was all she wanted to see.

"Almost there, almost there," she murmured. "Okay, stop!"

Enu hit the brake, and the truck shimmied and skidded on the dusty road.

"The border is immediately ahead of us," Kiandra said.

It just looked like more dry, flat land ahead, no different from the dry, flat land behind us. No—there was a small shimmering in the air, like the haze that shows up on an intensely hot day. But like a heat mirage, the shimmering didn't seem to stay in one place.

How were we supposed to get past something we couldn't properly see?

"I don't see any birds," Zeba murmured.

"Weren't you listening?" Kiandra said. "The Enforcers have exterminated as many of the birds out here as they can, because they mess up the border."

That was what Kiandra had found out, hacking into the Enforcers' own website about the border. The border rose high into the sky—meant to discourage even people trying to fly over it. Someone who flew a plane into the electrically charged border would only crash.

But birds, being smaller and more agile, didn't crash. Instead they repeatedly made the charge on the border short out.

If someone happened to cross the border at the exact right moment, just as a bird flew overhead, nothing would happen to that person. He or she might even believe that the border was gone. Because, for that one instant, it ceased to exist.

Enu had jokingly asked if Kiandra thought we could quickly train a bunch of birds to fly over our heads constantly. Kiandra said scornfully, "No, stupid. Though I'm sure that's the best *you* could come up with."

Her idea was that if someone threw rocks at just the right point of the border, that would have the same effect as birds.

"Are you sure this will work?" Enu asked Kiandra now, even as he drummed his fingers on the steering wheel.

"No, I'm not sure it will work," Kiandra snapped at him. "This is an untested scientific theory. I won't know if it works or not until we try it."

"Who's going to be the guinea pig?" Enu asked. "Before we try with the whole big truck, I mean . . ."

"I will," I said.

But I didn't reach for the door handle to get out of the truck. That shimmering haze that I could barely see was somehow scarier than a solid wall would have been.

But not scarier than if there were a row of fearsome Enforcers ready to attack us, I reminded myself. *And if you wait too long, maybe that's what will show up. They do patrols here, twice a day.*

Kiandra had dug up that little fact too. She'd also come up with pictures of the Enforcers in their dark, forbidding uniforms.

"I'll throw the rocks at the border while you walk through it," Zeba told me.

"Remember, she's got an awesome throw," Enu assumed me. "She won't hit you."

Did he have to give me something else to worry about?

But I yanked the door open and slipped down to the ground along with Zeba. She went around to the back of the truck and pulled out a large bag of rocks that we'd gathered from the side of the road, in the first stony area we'd found. Zeba opened the bag of rocks and winged one high into the sky. There was a soft sizzling sound, and for a split second I could see a grid of red lights—lasers, maybe?—that blinked out as soon as they appeared. If I hadn't been looking so closely, I might have thought the grid was an optical illusion, maybe just an odd reflection of the orange basketball shirt Zeba still wore.

"At least nothing exploded," I told Zeba.

"Are you sure you'll be safe doing this?" Zeba asked.

"Of course!" I lied.

I turned around and gave Enu and Kiandra the *okay* sign, my thumb and forefinger pressed confidently together. They still sat in the cab of the truck, and it occurred to me that it would be very easy for them to just drive off anytime they wanted.

"I'll throw this rock exactly the same," Zeba said, holding

one up. "Except the second it leaves my hand, I'll throw another one. And another. And another, until I see that you're through."

"I'll run and dive," I said. "And then—"

"Don't dive; jump," Zeba said. "Like you're doing the pencil jump, not a belly smacker, I mean. So you spend the least amount of time precisely in the border zone."

The pencil jump, I thought, and for a moment I was transported back to the Fredtown swimming pool, the sun beating down on my neck, the scratchy surface of the diving board rough beneath my feet as I ran toward the water. I *never* did the pencil jump. I was the one who dared all the other kids to try to make the biggest splash, smacking their arms, legs, bellies, or backs as hard as possible against the water.

Rosi was the one who liked the pencil jump. She could disappear under the water leaving barely a ripple behind.

I blinked hard and told Zeba, "It's now or never."

She reared back her arm, and I ran forward with my head cocked, watching the rock spinning overhead. I stayed precisely under it as I leaped, my arms pressed tightly to my side, my knees locked together, my legs as straight as I could make them. I saw a flash of red right before I landed. And then the rock started falling past me.

"You did it!" Zeba screamed. "You're across!"

I looked back at Enu and Kiandra, certain they'd be

clapping and cheering too. Maybe they'd even get out of the truck cab. It would probably be a little harder than this to get the truck across the border—Zeba would have to throw a *lot* of rocks, really fast. Enu or Kiandra would have to help her while the other one drove. Maybe I would too. But we'd do it. We'd get everyone and the truck across the border. And then we'd find Rosi, Bobo, and Cana. And then . . .

Enu and Kiandra were not clapping and cheering. They weren't even smiling. They were frowning and pointing off into the distance, far beyond me.

I turned around to see what they were pointing at. I squinted, trying to make sense of the billows of dust spinning at the horizon. I could make out three shapes—two much shorter than the first—and behind those shapes, a row of dark figures.

Kiandra shouted something. I don't know if the border distorted sound waves, or if my ears just weren't working right. But I had to shout back, "What? What did you say?"

This time her words reached me: distant, tinny—but understandable.

"Is that Rosi, Bobo, and Cana?" she called. "Being chased by Enforcers?"

CHAPTER
THIRTY-FOUR

"No!" I screamed. "We were supposed to find them before the Enforcers did! We were supposed to be able to smuggle them out without the Enforcers even knowing. . . ."

"Come back!" Zeba yelled at me from the other side of the border. "Come back, and we'll drive away before the Enforcers even see us!"

"What?" I called back to her. "And leave Rosi to be captured by the Enforcers?"

"How are you going to stop them?" she yelled. "What good does it do to have you captured too?"

I knew the Fred-approved answer to that: *None.* The Freds were all about self-sacrifice and helping others only when there was some value to the help and the sacrifice. Even their big dramatic Albert Schweitzer quote—*The purpose of human life is to serve, and to show compassion and the will to help others*—had to do with serving some purpose, accomplishing something.

But I wasn't like the Freds.

"I'm not turning around!" I yelled at Zeba.

"Please, please . . . ," Zeba called.

Out of the corner of my eye I could see Enu, still in the truck cab, waving his arm at Zeba and me.

"Get Edwy out of there!" he yelled at Zeba.

"Let's go!" Kiandra yelled.

I shook my head and started running. But I ran toward Rosi and the Enforcers, not back toward the truck.

"Edwy!" Zeba screamed behind me. "What are you doing?"

I thought I could hear Enu's voice again too, a bass rumble that blended with Zeba's higher-pitched shrieks. But I couldn't make out actual words—maybe because he was so far behind me now, on the other side of the border; maybe because the blood was pounding in my ears so dramatically as I ran, drowning out other sounds.

Then I heard the roar of the truck engine.

They're leaving me? I thought. *They're just driving away and leaving me—and Rosi and Bobo and Cana—in danger?*

What else should I have expected?

My feet kept slapping against the ground; I kept dashing toward the Enforcers and Rosi and the two little kids. How much time did I have before the Enforcers saw me? How much time did I have to come up with a plan?

Oddly, the roar of the truck engine seemed to get louder

and louder. I told myself it was some sort of sonic trick, some side effect of the border, taunting me. But it unnerved me enough that I glanced back over my shoulder, trying to sort out the sounds I heard behind me: not just the truck, but a constant thumping.

Enu was standing beside Zeba now, and they were both throwing rocks at the border.

As if that will do any good, I thought. *As if that will do anything but put them in danger for no reason . . .*

Then I saw that Kiandra was behind the wheel of the truck. She was revving the engine; she was speeding forward. . . .

She was crossing the border under the hail of Zeba and Enu's rocks.

She zoomed toward me, catching up easily. She had the windows down, and she screamed out at me, "Get in! We'll deal with those Enforcers together!"

CHAPTER
THIRTY-FIVE

I dragged myself over to the passenger side of the truck and climbed in. I panted hard—maybe just from running, maybe more from being surprised.

"Wh-why?" I asked, as soon as I could speak. "I thought you'd run away! Why didn't you?" A spark of hope ignited in my mind. "Do you have another brilliant plan?"

Kiandra winced.

"Not yet," she said. "But . . . I couldn't let you do this alone. Maybe I have started thinking of you as a little brother. One I have to protect."

"Hey!" I started to protest.

"Or . . . maybe I'm just as reckless and stupid as you are," she muttered. "Maybe you're *my* mini-me, not Enu's."

"Or you're my maxi-me," I countered. "I'm the original. You're the copy."

"Whatever," Kiandra said. "Doesn't matter now."

She pointed out the window: Two of the Enforcers had

turned their heads toward us. They knew we were here.

Kiandra hit the accelerator.

"By my calculations, we have about two minutes to come up with a plan," she said.

"Go faster!" I yelled at her. "Let's keep distracting the Enforcers! Before they capture Rosi and the two little kids! Or hurt them!"

Now that we were closer, I could see that the Enforcers held long sticklike shapes. But they weren't actually sticks—or any other type of weapon that could be used only if you were right beside a victim.

They were guns.

And those guns meant that we couldn't swing by, pick up Rosi, Bobo, and Cana, and drive off before the Enforcers had a chance to react.

They would shoot us all, if we tried that.

They could shoot any of us right now, if they wanted to.

"I think if they were planning to shoot your friends, they would have already done that," Kiandra said, as if she'd noticed the guns too and was trying to comfort me. She didn't speed up. "I bet the Enforcers are planning to trap your friends at the border. They want to take them alive. To interrogate them, just like their parents were interrogated."

"What?" I asked. "Why would they want to do that?"

And then suddenly I knew what information the

Enforcers might want from Rosi and the two little kids. I'd been slumped in my seat, but now I straightened up.

"Kiandra, I know you were probably checking things on your laptop while I was crossing the border," I said. "Did you see anything new? Any information that changed?"

"Um, no . . . ," Kiandra said.

She seemed to be struggling to keep the truck going at a steady pace, headed in a straight line. I remembered that, unlike Enu, she probably didn't even have video-game driving experience.

"Okay, okay," I said. "Just play along . . ."

We pulled up alongside the Enforcers. There were four of them: Two split off and pointed their guns at Kiandra and me. Two kept chasing Rosi, Bobo, and Cana.

To Rosi I yelled, "Run this way! Get in the truck!"

To the Enforcers I yelled, "Don't shoot anyone! I have information you need! I know . . . I know where your missing patroller is!"

CHAPTER THIRTY-SIX

Of course I was lying. But if I'm good at anything, it's lying.

Now I just had to make the Enforcers keep believing that lie until I figured out something else.

"Why are you here?" one of the Enforcers gasped.

"To help you find the patroller," I said impatiently, as if I were annoyed by his dimness. "The one who vanished from Cursed Town."

Now two Enforcers had their guns pointed only at me, not at Kiandra. But I pretended I didn't care.

"Edwy?" Rosi gasped, looking over her shoulder at me.

"One and the same," I said, reaching for all the cockiness I'd ever exhibited back in Fredtown.

Rosi turned and raced toward me, shepherding Bobo and Cana along with her. The Enforcers chasing her also turned.

Now there were four guns pointed in my direction.

Rosi acted as if she didn't care either. As soon as she got close, she flung herself at me.

"You kept your promise!" she cried.

"Yeah, there's a first time for everything," I muttered.

"No, really," she repeated, grabbing my shoulders. "You kept your promise to watch out for me! You came to find me!"

"Works both ways," I said. "You promised to watch out for me, too. And you were trying to do that, back in the marketplace. . . ."

"I was hoping to find you . . . ," Rosi murmured dazedly.

It was wonderful to see her, but she looked awful. She had always been—disgustingly—the neatest kid in the history of humanity. If she wore a dress with a bow, you could be sure that it was always tied perfectly, each side of the bow equally perky, the ends of the sash dangling the exact same length. Back in Fredtown I had never once seen her with a hair out of place; her dark curls were always under control or precisely pulled back into braids or a ponytail. I wasn't sure I'd ever seen her with so much as a smudge of dirt on her face.

But now her entire face was dirty. Her dress was ripped and practically in shreds at the hemline, as if she'd run through particularly sharp thorns and briars. Long, tangled strands of hair blew across her cheeks, and she made no attempt to push them back.

Still, her green eyes were as warm and hopeful as ever. That was what I wanted to keep looking at.

Rosi surprised me by wrapping her arms around me, drawing me into a hug. When her mouth was near my ear, she whispered, "Remember the fur? Your Fred-father's? Enforcers have something like that. Faces under mask faces. And they can't breathe if you knock off the masks."

What was she talking about? Was she just babbling nonsense? Had a week and a half as a fugitive in the wilderness made her lose her mind?

Then I remembered how I'd once tried to tell her that I suspected the Freds' faces hid something else underneath. She'd refused to believe me, back in Fredtown. *I* hadn't even quite believed my own eyes, until I'd talked to Enu and Kiandra about it.

But Rosi hadn't forgotten. And she believed me now.

She also knew that the Freds were aliens. That the Enforcers were too.

And did she think, now that I was here, the two of us could just rush around ripping the Enforcers' faces off?

I turned, back toward the Enforcers with their guns. I made myself imagine I was in one of Enu's video games.

If I took even a step toward the line of Enforcers, they would probably shoot.

I'd learned something from Enu's video games too.

"Is this boy telling the truth about our missing patroller?" one of the Enforcers asked the others.

"Do the scan," another said.

The first Enforcer pulled some sort of electronic device out of his uniform pocket and aimed it at me. I saw laserlike beams of red light coming toward me, and my first instinct was to jump out of the way. But by the time I'd had that thought, the Enforcer was already lowering the scanner; the light had already vanished.

Yeah, right, I thought. *It wasn't like I was going to move faster than the speed of light.*

The Enforcer looked down at the scanner and shook his head.

"The boy is lying," he said matter-of-factly, as if he was absolutely certain. As if his scanner was never wrong.

The other three Enforcers swung their guns toward me, as if I'd just become the one they hated the most.

I resisted the urge to call out, *Weren't you chasing Rosi? Isn't she the one you really want?*

I didn't know how else to stop the Enforcers from killing me. But I repeated to myself: *I won't betray Rosi. I will not be a coward when I die. I will be every bit as noble as any Fred ever tried to be. I'll be just like Albert Saintly Schweitzer, if I have to. But I won't be a coward!*

Then I heard a thud behind me: Kiandra jumping down from the truck.

"Oh, come on," she said. "How long have you even been

on Earth? A week and a half? How much contact have you really had with humans, when all you do is aim guns and bark orders? I bet that scanner was designed as a lie detector for your own species. Are you really that confident that human brain waves work the same as yours do, when we lie? What if the brain waves you're picking up only show that you're scaring the poor boy to death, pointing guns at him?"

I'd never been so grateful to have a big sister. But then she spoiled it by adding, "These kids were raised by *Freds*! All you have to do is raise your voice, and they think the world's ending. Look, why don't you check out what the boy's telling you, and *then* make up your minds about him?"

The Enforcers conferred, and I was disappointed that they did it in some language I didn't understand. That didn't give me anything to work with.

They also didn't stop pointing the guns at me. But I could imagine them shooting Kiandra or one of my friends just as easily. Whimpering, Bobo clutched Rosi's waist. A slow, silent tear crawled down Cana's face. Rosi clenched her teeth.

Finally one of the Enforcers grunted and muttered, "We'll check out the boy's story. You, boy, get into the cab of the truck and tell us where to go. The rest of you—get into the back of the truck. Now!"

He nudged Rosi's ribs with the end of his gun. One of the

other Enforcers did the same to Kiandra. A third Enforcer scooped up Cana and Bobo as carelessly as if he were gathering up sticks or garbage—items he wouldn't care about harming.

"Okay, okay, we'll do as you say—just don't hurt the little ones!" Rosi gasped. "They're innocent! I forced them to come with me, I—"

One of the Enforcers put his hand over her mouth and dragged her around to the back of the truck.

I watched helplessly as the Enforcer grabbed Kiandra as well.

"Give Rosi a hug!" I called after her. "Comfort each other!" Because maybe then Rosi could tell Kiandra how to stop the Enforcers, just like she'd told me. Maybe only one Enforcer would climb into the back of the truck, and Rosi, Kiandra, Bobo, and Cana could overpower him.

But then I heard the Enforcer standing by me call out, "Standard troop positions, men. Two in the back of the truck, two in the cab."

Rosi, Kiandra, Bobo, and Cana wouldn't dare try to overpower two Enforcers. They *shouldn't* dare to try that.

The Enforcer beside me jerked on my arm, shoving me into the cab of the truck. He slid in beside me and grabbed the steering wheel. Another Enforcer went around to the other side and climbed in. I was trapped between them.

There was no way I could overpower both of the Enforcers surrounding me, either. There was no reason I should try.

I heard the door slam shut at the back of the truck, and something—a fist maybe?—thudded against one of the truck walls. It must have been a signal that the Enforcers in the back had everyone in place and were ready to go.

My heart sank. I hadn't been a coward. But the only thing I'd accomplished, with all my bravery, was that I'd helped the Enforcers capture Rosi, Bobo, Cana—and even Kiandra—and provided a truck for the Enforcers to trap them in.

What was I supposed to do now?

CHAPTER
THIRTY-SEVEN

"You and your friend came from the other side of the border," the Enforcer behind the steering wheel growled at me as he reached down and started the truck's engine. "I saw you coming from that direction. How did you get across?"

Lie again? I thought. *Tell him his vision was bad?*

How was I supposed to convince him he couldn't trust his own eyes?

"Border? What border?" I asked, hoping I sounded just as I always did to my Fred-parents when I whined, *Cookie? What cookie? Why are you accusing me of eating the last cookie?* Or to my Fred-teachers, *Homework? What homework? I think you forgot to make the assignment. It's not fair to blame me!*

No, scratch that. My Fred-parents and my Fred-teachers never really believed me. I had to make the Enforcers think I was just stupid and ignorant enough to not even know I'd crossed the border.

"Do you mean . . . oh, there was this kind of weird flash of red light," I said. "But I thought it was an optical illusion, because there was a flock of birds flying above me, kind of making weird patterns in the sunlight. . . ."

"I thought we killed all the birds," the second Enforcer grumbled.

I shrugged.

"I'm just telling you what I saw," I said, as if I didn't understand why it would matter.

"So tell us where you saw the patroller," the first Enforcer said as he put the truck into gear.

"It's hard to explain," I said. "I think I'd do better showing you. Turn around and go that way." I pointed behind us, back toward the border.

The Enforcer grunted. The truck shivered and the engine sputtered, as if he'd shifted gears too quickly.

"Curses on the humans' primitive technology," he muttered.

"We do the best we can," I said, adding belatedly, "sir."

Would it help to make him think I was totally in awe of his superiority and power?

I *was* totally in awe of his superiority and power. And of the gun the second Enforcer held, pinning me against the seat. It made my brain numb.

"Perhaps humans and Enforcers can work their way

toward getting along a little bit better," I said, sounding as prim and foolishly optimistic as a Fred. "Perhaps one day we'll even share our technology, back and forth, each helping the other. Perhaps we just got off on the wrong foot, and the longer we're around each other, the more we'll—"

The Enforcer on my right jabbed the end of his gun into my ribs.

"We have no desire to get along with humans," he said. "Or to share anything. We're not Freds. We know your limitations. We don't like you. You are not even worthy opponents to hunt."

To hunt? No, no, no, no . . . , my brain screamed.

I had to think about something else. Surely there was a way out of this. Surely I'd find it soon. Surely there was enough time. . . .

The truck was going fast enough now that the Enforcer driving it wouldn't have to worry about shifting gears anymore. We were almost to the border. Without moving my head, I glanced around for Enu and Zeba. Would they still be there waiting to throw rocks at the border, letting Kiandra and me back through?

They were nowhere in sight. I told myself that was good— it was better for them if they'd hidden somewhere. But I also felt lonely. Abandoned.

"So, this border you were talking about," I said, turning

toward the Enforcer on my left. "Is it something you worry about crossing too?"

"Enforcers never worry about anything," he growled. "We've got nothing *to* worry about."

We were close enough to the border now that I could see it shimmer. Was this some kind of test? Was he waiting for me to point it out?

What *would* happen to a human trying to speed through the border in a truck without birds overhead? What if going through the border like this was something that could hurt or kill a human, but have no effect whatsoever on an Enforcer?

I didn't actually know for sure. I didn't know much of anything. Why hadn't I asked Kiandra more questions when I had the chance?

I was almost out of time. The front bumper of the truck was about to hit the shimmering border. But just then the Enforcer on my right pulled out the same kind of small electronic device the other man had used as a lie detector. He hit some button on the device, and we sped right through the border as if it weren't even there.

As soon as we were on the other side, he hit the button again.

I have to get my hands on one of those devices, I thought.

The Enforcer slipped it back into his pocket and went back to sticking his gun in my side.

"Where to?" the other Enforcer growled at me.

"Th-there," I said, pointing toward the rock formation where we'd left Udans.

If I couldn't think of anything better, maybe I could tell them I'd thought Udans was the missing patroller. Maybe the Enforcers wouldn't punish him—or me—too severely for that.

But that still didn't save Rosi, Bobo, or Cana from the Enforcers.

Or Kiandra, I reminded myself. *Or me. You've just added to the number of people in danger. . . .*

Directing the Enforcers toward Udans would at least buy some time. Right now, that was the best I could do.

The Enforcer sped up, covering the distance back to the rock formation in no time at all. We rounded the corner, and the signpost where we'd left Udans came into sight.

The sign still pointed toward Refuge City. And a rope still dangled from the post, right where Enu had tied it. But the other end of the rope trailed off into the dust.

Udans was nowhere to be seen.

CHAPTER
THIRTY-EIGHT

Okay, then, you don't have to worry about putting Udans in danger, I told myself. *At least he'll be fine.*

But with the Enforcer's gun digging into my side, I couldn't bring myself to care that much about Udans's safety.

Enu! I wanted to scream. *Were you too busy playing video games to ever learn how to tie knots well? Did you ever think that it might really, really matter?*

What could I tell the Enforcers now? What lie could I come up with when I didn't even have Udans to point to?

"Now what?" the driver growled at me.

"Slow down so I can see where we are," I mumbled.

I was stalling. I had sweat trickling down my face, and I was sure the Enforcers were about to realize that that was what humans did when they lied. Some of the sweat got into my eyes, blurring my vision.

Or maybe I was crying.

That time when Udans kidnapped me, I'd been so

flippant about everything. I'd made it a joke, that his hands smelled like puke.

Maybe, straight from Fredtown, I hadn't really understood what true danger was.

Or maybe, because he was actually protecting me, just doing my father's bidding, I'd been able to tell deep down that he really didn't want to hurt me.

This was different. The Enforcers didn't care if they hurt me. Or if they hurt Rosi, Bobo, Cana, or Kiandra. They didn't care if they hurt every human on the planet.

This was true danger. I was in danger—and all my friends and family were too.

The entire planet was in danger.

"You don't know anything about our patroller, do you, kid?" the Enforcer who was driving growled at me. "You've been lying to us from the start, haven't you?"

I wiped the sweat (or tears) out of my eyes and turned my head to face him. The rock formation towered just outside his window. About halfway up on the formation, I saw a dark spot—maybe a cave, maybe just an indentation.

"Stop!" I cried to Enforcer. "I know where we are now! The patroller's hiding in that cave! I'll lead you to him!"

It was another desperate lie, but the Enforcer grunted and hit the brake. All three of us got out of the cab, the second Enforcer keeping the gun against my ribs the whole time. My feet skidded on pebbles mixed in with the sandy soil under my feet.

If I could distract one of the Enforcers, even for an instant, would that be enough time for me to bend down, pick up a pebble, and throw it at the other Enforcer's face fast enough to knock his mask off? I wondered. *And then would I have time to attack the other Enforcer too?*

It would require absolutely perfect throws. It would require hitting the exact right point on the Enforcers' faces on my first try. That is, if I could find the exact right point at all. When I'd jarred my Fred-father's face and seen a flash of blue fur that made me curious, it had been nothing but an accident. I hadn't been aiming.

And, anyhow, what if the Freds and the Enforcers were just different enough that what I remembered as the right point on my Fred-father's face wasn't a mask-release spot for an Enforcer?

The Enforcers stayed side by side. They kept their guns pointed precisely at my back.

Then one muttered something into his electronic device. The back door of the truck opened, and the other two Enforcers stepped out. I tried to see in, to get a glimpse of Rosi, Bobo, Cana or Kiandra, to see how they were doing, but the Enforcers shut the door too quickly.

They locked it too, so no one could escape.

Now I had four Enforcers behind me, four guns trained on my back.

"Y-you just have to climb up this way," I stammered, heading toward the rock formation.

The pebbles and rocks slid around under my feet, and it was a struggle to stay upright. If I let myself fall, could I gather up a handful of rocks and throw them really, really fast at all four Enforcers?

I hadn't even thought I'd be able to knock out two Enforcers before one of them shot me. There was absolutely no way I could hit twice that many. Even Enu with his video-game reflexes and skill couldn't have done that.

Oh, Enu, I thought, and it was silly, but I kind of wished I'd told him he'd been a fun big brother. Even if he'd only ever invited me to play basketball because he'd run out of other choices, I was glad he'd let me play.

I really should have been thinking of a good plan while I climbed higher and higher through the rocks, but my mind balked at that just as much as I'd ever balked at what the Freds wanted me to do, back in Fredtown. Instead my mind kept listing all the good-byes and thank-yous I'd probably never be able to say.

Oh, Kiandra, I thought. *I wish there'd been time for you to teach me everything you know about computers. Oh, Zeba, I hope you get safely back to Refuge City. Oh, Rosi. Rosi, Rosi,*

Rosi. I hope you'll remember me as the kid who tried to rescue you. Not as the kid who dyed your hair with Kool-Aid back in Fredtown. Or threw shaving-cream pies at you. Or . . .

Well. No need to list every prank I'd ever played on Rosi. Not when the Enforcers were probably going to shoot me when we got up to that cave and no one was there.

You forgive me, don't you, Rosi? I thought.

I didn't actually have to ask her this question directly. It was like I already had my answer, from the hug she'd given me.

"Is that the cave you are leading us toward?" one of the Enforcers behind me asked.

I turned around to see where he was pointing. Even in my terror I was tempted to say, *Well, duh! Do you see more than one cave?*

It was nice to know that I was still capable of at least *thinking* sarcastic thoughts.

But as I turned, I noticed that there was actually a second darker area above me, off to the side, narrower than the cave I'd seen from down below. I raised up on my tiptoes, trying to see which indentation in the rock face was deeper, which cave would buy me more time.

In the first cave I saw a flash of orange.

My heart almost stopped.

I climbed a step higher, giving me a clearer view of the

first cave. It really was barely more than a cavelike indentation in the rock face. It was shielded from the Enforcers' view by a row of boulders right at the cave's mouth. But I was close enough now to understand the flash of orange I'd seen:

It was Enu's basketball T-shirt.

And Enu, Zeba, and Udans were all cowering behind the boulders.

CHAPTER
THIRTY-NINE

No, no, no, no! screamed in my head. *What am I supposed to do now? Why didn't I realize these three might be hiding here? Why didn't I lead the Enforcers somewhere else?*

But there was nowhere else anyone might have gone to hide around here *except* the rock formation.

Udans pressed his finger over his lips and shook his head frantically at me.

I turned back to the Enforcers.

"Oh, you thought it was *that* cave?" I said loudly, pointing toward the boulders Enu, Zeba, and Udans were cowering behind. "I'm actually headed toward *that* one."

I pointed off to the side. My hand shook so much, there was no way the Enforcers could make sense of where I was pointing.

And the other cave was too shallow. There was no way the Enforcers would believe anyone was hidden there. They could probably see that, even from where they stood, four steps behind me.

How much time did I have before they just decided to shoot me? At what point was it last-minute enough that I could dive for the ground and just start throwing rocks—because everything else was hopeless?

"Nadrik?" the lead Enforcer called toward the shallow cave. I guess that was the lost patroller's name. But the word only echoed hollowly against the rocks, and the Enforcer looked back at me. "Why does he not answer us?"

"He . . . he was unconscious when I saw him," I said. "That's why I was going to get help. I knew I couldn't carry him down from here all by myself."

"You had that girl with you," the lead Enforcer growled back at me.

"Yes, but I didn't think even two of us could carry him," I said. "We're kids, remember?"

Would they think, *Oh, that's right. We can't shoot kids?*

No. They wouldn't. I could tell by their faces. Or—their masks.

It was so frustrating that I knew the secret to overpowering the Enforcers, but I couldn't use it because I was alone. I couldn't get anyone to help me. It was like being back in Fredtown, when I felt like I was the only one trying to find out the truth.

But eventually, once we were in Cursed Town, Rosi had wanted to know the truth as much as I did. I had never been as alone as I thought I was.

And I wasn't actually entirely alone now. It was just that Rosi, Bobo, Cana, and Kiandra were trapped. And Udans, Enu, and Zeba weren't in any position to help me with my lies.

What if I tried truth instead?

I turned back to the Enforcers.

"Is it true," I asked in my loudest voice, "that you Enforcers have a weakness? That if someone hits you at the exact right place on your jaw, your faces come off and you can't breathe?"

All four of the Enforcers aimed their guns more precisely— at the exact spot on my chest where nothing but ribs and muscle and skin protected my frantically beating heart.

"Now where would you have heard that?" the lead Enforcer asked in an icy voice.

"Oh, it's just a rumor going around," I said. I held my hands up, a gesture of innocence. "Not that I could do anything by myself, of course. Not when there are four of you and only one of me. Why, I'd need at least three friends to help me out, to even have a chance to do anything. . . ."

I wanted so badly to look back at the boulders, to see if Udans, Enu, and Zeba understood what I was really saying.

To see if they were brave enough. To see if they knew what all of humanity needed us to do.

There was so much I didn't know, so much I didn't understand. But I finally had a plan.

I threw myself at the ground and screamed, "Now!"

CHAPTER FORTY

I heard nothing but gunfire.

Udans, Enu, and Zeba didn't hear me, or they didn't understand, I thought. *Or they don't care. And I'm going to die.*

After a moment of stark terror, I decided maybe I wouldn't die immediately. Maybe the Enforcers were shooting just to scare me, not to actually injure me, because none of the bullets hit my body, even as they pinged off rocks all around me. The gunfire continued, but I dared to turn my head and look toward the sky.

A rock sailed between me and the clouds.

"Thank you!" I screamed. "Thank you, thank you, thank you—"

The rocks kept flying. The gunfire got softer, as if there'd been four guns firing, and now there were only three. And then it was softer still—was it possible that now there were only one or two?

And then the gunfire ended, and all I could hear was the thudding of rocks.

CHAPTER
FORTY-ONE

I was still cowering on the ground when I felt a hand on my back. Someone screamed in my ear, but for a moment all I could hear was the echo of gunshots and falling rocks. Then the sound made sense to me. It was Enu's hand on my back and his voice yelling, "Edwy, you're safe! Where's Kiandra? What happened to her?"

My arms and legs shook as I pushed myself up.

"She's locked in the back of the truck," I told him. "She's all right. At least, I think she's all right. . . ."

I glanced down toward the truck, still parked sideways by the signpost where we'd once tied Udans—ages ago, millennia ago. Between me and the truck, four dark shapes lay strewn across the rocks. Their faces looked askew. Did they have antennae sticking out from underneath their fake, human-looking faces? And did their real faces have ridges by their eyes, like beetles might?

I didn't care what the Enforcers really looked like, as

long as they didn't move. I saw Udans scramble past me, toward the fallen bodies, and I threw my arms around Enu. I couldn't help it. I was raised by Freds. And no matter how I fought it, they had taught me to thank people who did great things for me.

"You understood what I was telling you to do!" I cried. "You and Zeba and Udans knocked out the Enforcers! I think you just saved my life! Or, at least, saved me from being the Enforcers' prisoner for the rest of my life . . ."

Enu flushed.

"Edwy—it was all Udans, throwing those rocks," he said. "Zeba and me, we were too scared."

I could barely believe it. And I could barely believe that tough, swaggering Enu would admit he'd been afraid.

"Just Udans?" I mumbled, stunned. "You mean . . . one person was able to do all of that? You mean if I had only tried, I could have. . . ."

Udans looked up from where he was bent over the nearest Enforcer.

"You could not have hit them all before they shot you, because you were out in the open," he told me. "I could risk it only because I had the boulders hiding me. And Enu and Zeba handing me rocks. And you shouting about hitting their faces."

"I still should have been brave enough to throw one," Zeba

whispered. She'd crept up beside Enu and me, and I hadn't even noticed. Tears streamed down her face. I noticed that.

"I just kept thinking," she went on, "what if they kill me? What if I kill one of them? How would I live with that?"

Udans kept gazing at us.

"You are children," he said. "None of you have been through a war. You have never before had to think like a soldier." Enu started to protest—he probably wanted to say something about video games—but Udans silenced him with a stern glance.

"Until now, you have never had to think like a *real* soldier, in a real battle," Udans amended. "And, God willing, you will never have to think that way again. But I fear . . ."

Zeba and Enu both huddled beside me. Enu didn't push my hands down from his shoulders, like I expected. Zeba drew her knees to her chest and wrapped her arms around her legs, as if she was trying to make her body as small as possible.

I think we were all in shock.

"Are those Enforcers dead?" Zeba asked in a quiet voice.

"Do you want them to be?" Udans asked.

"Yes . . . no . . . The Freds taught us all life is valuable," Zeba said. "But . . ."

"*I* want them dead," Enu said.

Udans pulled something out of his shirt pocket. A vial and a needle.

"It is the girl who will get her wish," he said. Quickly he put the needle into the vial and then used it to inject each one of the Enforcers in turn. Then he tugged at the Enforcer's faces, pulling their human masks—their breathing apparatus—back into place.

"This ensures that they will be unconscious for the next twelve hours," he said. "But they will not die. There are people in Refuge City who will be eager to study their bodies, eager to keep them imprisoned the way they would like to imprison us."

"Udans—did *you* have something to do with the patroller the Enforcers have been looking for?" I ask. "Did you maybe smuggle him to Refuge City too?"

His face looked as rocklike as my father's ever had.

"I tried," he said. "Your father and I and . . . some others in Cursed Town. We tried to get that patroller to the scientists in the city. But we didn't know the proper way to handle Enforcers. That man died. The scientists had to do a chemical analysis to find out why."

"Udans, you're not a country bumpkin," Enu said. "You're a hero!"

"It is possible for me to be both at once," Udans said. The corners of his mouth twitched. In a less grim moment it might have even been called a smile.

I guess even Udans didn't believe there was *nothing* he

could do to change the world. I guess he just did it . . . secretly. While telling us kids we couldn't do anything.

"Help me move these bodies," he said, lifting one Enforcer by the shoulders. "Their spy sensors probably detected the gunfire. And other Enforcers are probably coming to investigate right now. . . . Let's be elsewhere when they arrive, all right?"

I almost fell over when I tried to stand, but Udans got us all moving down through the rocks. Enu picked up the guns and handed them to Zeba. She looked like just touching them would make her throw up, but she took them without comment. Udans tugged two Enforcers downhill, over the rocky slope. Enu and I each dragged one. But when we got close to the truck, I couldn't help myself: I dropped the Enforcer and grabbed the lever to unlock and open the back liftgate of the truck.

Rosi and Kiandra stood just inside the door, poised to spring out at any Enforcers nearby. Cana and Bobo were back by the boxes, as if they'd been told to hide and be safe, but neither of them could stay put.

"You! Where—? What—? The Enforcers—?" Rosi couldn't even finish one question before she started another one.

"It's okay, Rosi," I said. "Everyone's okay. We're all safe now."

EPILOGUE

We rode back into Refuge City feeling like triumphant heroes. Of course, Udans, Enu, and Kiandra had to explain to the rest of us exactly what it meant to be a triumphant hero, because it wasn't something the Freds had taught us about.

But we were triumphant. And Udans had kindly told us that we'd all acted heroically, even if we'd all had moments of being scared.

"You think I am not scared sometimes too?" he asked.

"We know you are," Enu said quickly. "But now we understand why."

Because we couldn't fit everyone in the cab of the truck, Enu and Kiandra rode up front with Udans, while Zeba, Rosi, Bobo, Cana, and I rode in the back, sitting on boxes arranged in a circle.

We didn't mean to divide up based on who had been raised in a Fredtown and who hadn't. But that was how it worked out.

The unconscious Enforcers were stowed in the secret compartment, under the box I sat on. They barely fit. But, still, there were four of them—maybe the space was slightly bigger than it had seemed when I was trapped there myself.

Udans had worried that alarms would go off when the Ref City scanners detected the Enforcers' presence, and that reminded me that Rosi, Bobo, and Cana didn't have the right papers either. But Kiandra assured us all that she could hack into the system and jam the city scanners. She made it sound easy.

I trusted Kiandra. But it was hard to forget about the Enforcers beneath my feet, all the way back to Refuge City.

As I might have expected, Rosi and Zeba hit it off famously.

"It's nice to meet another twelve-year-old girl," Rosi said hesitantly, smiling through the dirt on her face.

"Don't worry—Kiandra's all about girl power too," I said. "She'll tell you all about it."

"Why would anyone talk about 'girl power' or 'boy power' when we're all humans?" Rosi asked, at the same time that Zeba said, "Doesn't talking about one person's power imply that there would be someone else who might not have power? Isn't that dangerous?"

Yeah, it was pretty clear that they were going to be friends.

But then Rosi turned to me and said, "I missed you."

Bobo sidled up beside me and leaned his head on my shoulder, almost as if he were my little brother too.

"Yeah, so many times when we were walking, Rosi would say, 'Think about how Edwy would jump over that log' or 'Can't you be a brave big boy like Edwy?'" Bobo said. "I even made up a song about it: 'Edwy, Edwy, Edwy, Edwy's always the best. . . .'"

"I don't think Edwy wants to hear you sing right now, Bobo," Rosi said. Even in the dim light of the closed-in truck, I could see her face redden. "Remember, it's not polite to sing while others are trying to talk."

This was such a perfectly prissy *Rosi* thing to say, I almost laughed out loud.

Rosi still had dirt on her face, and her hair looked like she'd come through a cyclone. I'd seen her try to smooth it down, but after a week and a half of being a fugitive in the wilderness, she needed more help than that. She still looked almost nothing like the Rosi I'd been used to back in Fredtown.

But she looked absolutely beautiful. I even kind of understood now why Enu talked about how pretty girls were.

Cana leaned on my knee on the opposite side from Bobo.

"Do you still disagree with everything about the Freds?" she asked plaintively. "Don't you ever miss Fredtown?"

"Sometimes I do," I admitted. "But it wasn't where we belonged. Things weren't *real* there."

"Are things real in Refuge City?" Cana asked in her wise little five-year-old-girl voice. "Were things real in Cursed Town?" I winced, because the name sounded so much worse coming from an innocent little kid. We probably shouldn't have talked about Cursed Town in front of her and Bobo. But they'd been there. They'd seen what it was like. "Was it real when the Enforcers were chasing us?"

"Um . . . ," I floundered.

"What Edwy means," Rosi interrupted, "is that the Freds were kind of playing make-believe in Fredtown. They were pretending there weren't any bad things in the universe we'd ever have to deal with."

"But we will," Zeba whispered.

"There are bad things out there we have to fix," Rosi said firmly. "Edwy and his brother and sister—and Udans and Zeba—they all rescued us from some bad things by the border. And now we have to find a way to rescue all the other kids left behind in Cursed Town."

I looked down at my feet. I knew that the Enforcers were right below, unconscious and defeated for now, but only for now. Our victory was a temporary one.

"Rosi's wrong," I said, and when she started to protest, I stared her down. "It's not just the kids in Cursed Town we have to rescue—it's all the people there. The grown-ups, too. And in all the other towns like it. We have to help all of humanity."

Rosi started to giggle.

"Oh, Edwy," she said. "Edwy, Edwy, Edwy. I never thought I'd hear you sounding so much like a Fred."

"I don't sound like a Fred," I told her. "I've got bigger dreams than they ever did. Bigger goals. I want to help *everyone*."

I wanted to hear what Rosi would say to that, but just then the truck abruptly shuddered to a halt. I almost fell over backward. The box under me skidded sideways. Rosi and Zeba slammed against the wall.

Someone hit the back door, and it began sliding open.

"Get out! Get out!" Kiandra screamed at us when there was still just a crack between the bottom of the door and the floor of the truck. "I just figured out how to monitor the Enforcers' conversations on this device!" She held up one of the pocket-sized scanners the Enforcers had used. "They've got a tracker on us! They say the fact that four of their Enforcers were carried off—that means they're entitled to take over Refuge City, too! We can't let them find us with the captured Enforcers!"

I scrambled out, pulling Bobo along with me. Rosi carried Cana, and Zeba helped her down. Kiandra pulled the back door of the truck shut behind us. Then Enu pulled us all back toward the curb.

After the dim interior of the truck, I stood blinking in the bright lights of a typical Ref City street. I heard Bobo murmur, "Oh, cool!" Rosi and Cana just gazed around, their eyes huge with awe.

The truck pulled away from us.

"Wait—Udans is staying with the truck?" I asked.

"He said he has to get it far away from us, so the Enforcers won't make the connection," Kiandra whispered. "Oh, Edwy, he's sacrificing himself for us. . . ."

Udans the kidnapper, I thought. *The pirate. And now he's been a hero twice in one day. . . .*

"And for now Kiandra's jamming every bioscan system she can, but we don't know how long that will last," Enu said. "We've got to find someplace to hide before the Enforcers get here, someplace that isn't our apartment or Zeba's soup kitchen. . . ."

The truck disappeared into traffic. All seven of us kids began blindly scrambling in the opposite direction, through the crowds. We'd gone barely a block when I noticed the people around me had stopped. They were all staring up at an enormous news screen on the side of the nearest building, with the words *Emergency announcement! Emergency announcement!* scrolling across it.

A booming voice cried out from loudspeakers all around us, "Due to a violent uprising near Refuge City, the Enforcers are being sent in to take control of all the formerly free zones, as covered in the terms of Agreement 5062. We repeat, the Enforcers are now in the process of taking control of the whole planet. . . ."

Everyone around me looked dazed. But I gathered the other six kids close to me.

"We'll be okay," I said. "Don't worry! We'll just tell everyone in Ref City that there's a way to disable the Enforcers. We'll tell the secret about the Enforcers' faces and the masks, and they won't be able to take over. We've just got to get the word out! Kiandra, can't you take over that public announcement system?"

Kiandra's eyes lit up, and she started to nod. But then she looked past me, back toward the screen.

"Too late," she whispered, pointing.

On the screen, a row of Enforcers were marching into what I recognized as the outskirts of Refuge City. They looked almost exactly like the Enforcers we'd encountered out in the wilderness: same dark uniforms, same grim expressions.

But over their heads they all wore clear, bubble-shaped helmets—helmets that covered their vulnerable faces completely.

"They know what we did out in the wilderness," Kiandra whispered. "They've already adapted."

Around us people were weeping. People were screaming. People were bashing their heads against the nearest wall.

"Don't people know that's not a good idea?" Bobo asked in his innocent little-boy voice.

I swallowed hard. I couldn't let him down, any more than I could have let Rosi down.

"They just don't know what else to do," I told Bobo. "But they're going to be all right. Because we're going to think of something better to do. We will. We're going to fix everything."

"We will," Rosi whispered, as if all the disagreements we'd ever had were over.

It was like we'd been on the same team all along.

We were definitely on the same team now.

TURN THE PAGE
FOR A SNEAK PEEK AT
CHILDREN OF JUBILEE

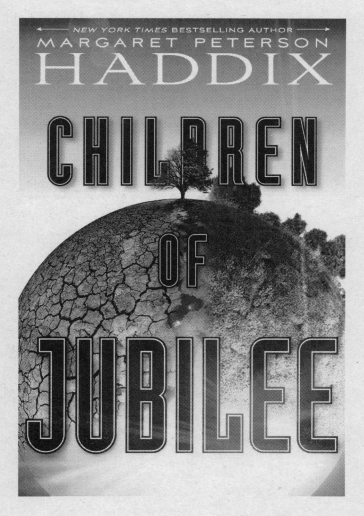

"Run! Hide!" my brother Enu screamed beside me.

Enu had been trying to boss me around my whole life. Usually I resisted. But the sound I'd thought was thunder kept striking louder and louder behind us. It was the sound of marching feet.

Enforcers' marching feet.

Coming toward us.

I leaned forward, bent my knees, and shoved off the pavement, trying to launch myself through a gap in the crowd ahead.

This is not my life, I thought.

I was a tech geek. A coder. A hacker. A *Why leave the couch when everything's available online?* type. I never ran.

A hand grabbed my arm from behind.

"We have to stay together!" someone yelled.

Edwy. My *little* brother. The brother I'd never met until a few weeks ago. The one who'd always been kept safe.

Until . . . well, a few weeks ago.

"We need you!" he begged. Because I guess I was still barreling forward.

Oh, momentum . . . It's not just a scientific theory.

I whirled around. There must have been hundreds of people around us scrambling to escape. Maybe thousands. Maybe the entire population of Refuge City. But I got something like tunnel vision: My eyes could focus only on five faces. Three belonged to twelve-year-olds: Edwy and his friends Rosi and Zeba. Two belonged to five-year-olds: Rosi's little brother, Bobo, and a girl named Cana. Until a few weeks ago I'd never seen such young children in person, not since I was that age myself. When, of course, being that little seemed natural. But now it was hard to believe that such tiny human beings as five-year-olds were real. They seemed more like dolls or toys.

"Kiandra, will you carry me?" Cana asked, raising her arms to me. "I'm scared."

Me too, kid, I thought.

"Enu's the one with muscles," I said, backing away from her. Where was Enu?

He'd shoved his way farther into the crowd ahead of us than I had, but I grabbed for his hand and jerked him back. Because suddenly it hit me that Edwy was right: We did need to stick together. With the Enforcers invading Refuge City, we wouldn't be able to find one another electronically. How much longer would it be safe to use anything electronic at all?

Not . . . able . . . to . . . use . . . electronics. . . .

It was a horrifying thought. I glanced down at the stolen Enforcer communication device in my hand. We'd taken it from one of the Enforcers we'd battled out in the desert. I was *mostly* confident that I'd managed to disable any tracking built into the device, just as I was *mostly* confident that I'd blocked all the bioscans for the entire city, so the seven of us kids wouldn't instantly be picked up as criminals.

Now would be a really bad time to be wrong.

"I want *you* to carry me, Kiandra," Cana insisted, grabbing my waist.

Now, what was that about? Granted, Bobo had already hopped up into Rosi's arms, so she wasn't available. But Cana had known Edwy her entire life—why wasn't he her first choice? Or Zeba, who liked taking care of people? Or Enu, who really did have a lot of muscles and could have carried Cana on his back without even noticing?

Cana wasn't the only one staring at me with wide, terrified eyes. Rosi, Zeba, Edwy, and now even Enu were too. And Bobo probably would have, except that he'd just buried his face against his sister's neck, letting her stare for both of them.

Oh. Everybody thinks I have a plan. Everyone thinks I can save them.

I tucked the Enforcer communication device under my arm and pulled out my mobile phone.

"We need to find the best hiding place," I told Enu. "*Before* we start running."

Someone or something—Enu? Zeba? Just the natural pressure of the screaming, fleeing crowd?—pushed us to the side, against the wall of a Ref City skyscraper. But I was lost in an electronic world, searching for maps of all the nearby basements. Type, type, swipe, maximize, minimize. . . . Just in case someone could track my search, I clicked on a building four blocks to the east, even as I announced to the group, "Follow me. We're going west."

Cana grabbed my shoulders and scrambled up onto my back—okay, whatever. I pulled the Enforcer communication device from beneath my arm and handed it to her.

"Hide this between us," I told her, and she obediently tucked it under her chin, against my back.

But then I felt bad, like I was endangering her too much. She was *five*.

I was so not used to watching out for anyone but myself.

We reached a deserted alleyway full of Dumpsters.

"The door at the end!" I shouted, pointing. "I hacked in and changed the security code for the keypad to eight-zero-nine-two. Go!"

I twisted around to pull Cana from my back and hand her to Enu. She held on tighter.

"Aren't you coming with us?" Cana asked.

No, not just Cana—Enu practically whimpered the same thing. Maybe the others did too. My ears had starting ringing so badly I could barely hear anything.

I broke Cana's hold on me and thrust her at Enu.

"After I hide this!" I yanked the Enforcer communication device from between Cana and me as it fell. "We don't want to be caught with it!"

Enu grabbed my wrist.

"We get caught, we're doomed anyway," he said. "We can't lose you."

This was the worst thing ever. Not the doomed part—I already knew that. It was Enu being sentimental and needy that slayed me. He'd spent the past thirteen years—my entire life—pretty much saying, "Why do I have to have a little sister? Sisters are useless! Why couldn't you have been the banished one? Why couldn't I have a brother instead?"

And then, just a matter of weeks ago, Edwy had shown up at our door.

Now look where we were: homeless fugitives, desperately fleeing the alien Enforcers.

And the Enforcers claimed they had the right to take over Ref City just because of something *we'd* done.

I wanted to make a joke about all this, to wisecrack, *Who's useless now?* I wanted all this to *be* a joke. Enu and me, we didn't do serious.

But this day was nothing but serious.

"I'm not going far," I said, my voice gruff. "I'll just hide it . . . over there."

I gestured at one of the Dumpsters. Strategically, this was really dumb. If the Dumpster was ever emptied again—if Ref City ever became that normal again—the communication device would be taken away. And it was insanity to keep the device in the same alleyway where we were hiding. How hard could it be to stash the device in the next alley over? Or—even better—a block or two away?

But I gazed out of the alley at the hordes flooding past on the street. Just in the few seconds since we'd ducked past the Dumpsters, the crowd had gone from panicked to frenzied to rabid. People were knocking one another down. People were trampling other people's bodies.

"Bobo and Cana can't see this," Rosi said. Her brother still had his face burrowed against her neck, but she put her hand on Cana's head, gently steering the younger girl to look toward the door leading to safety. "Come on."

She tugged Enu and Cana toward the door. Once Enu started moving, Rosi pulled Edwy and Zeba after them.

Zeba peered at me, her eyes wide with shock and horror.

"Kiandra, please—" she began.

"I'll be right behind you," I promised. I wanted to add, *Believe me, I'm no martyr. I know how to look out for number one.*

But that wasn't actually something I could promise. Not today.

I crouched low to hide in the shadow of the Dumpsters, and dashed to the nearest one. Then I slid the Enforcer communication device into the gap between the bottom of the Dumpster and the ground. Nobody would see it there.

Unless some rat comes along and noses it out into the open, I thought. *Unless . . .*

"Kiandra!"

Enu stood in the doorway at the end of the alley. I could see the others behind him, descending the stairs into darkness.

Should have stopped to grab flashlights, I thought. *Should have studied survival tips for life on the streets.*

I really hated situations I wasn't prepared for. Situations I couldn't study and analyze ahead of time.

But maybe my feet were smarter than my brain, because I started sprinting toward Enu and the doorway. When I was still a meter or two away, he reached out and pulled me in. The metal door began swinging shut behind us.

"Wait," I said, when there was only a narrow crack left between the door and the frame.

"Did you hear something? Is someone there?" Enu hissed at me. He was already three steps down the stairs. The others were far below. "Shut the door! Lock it!"

I hadn't heard anything new. I'd *stopped* hearing

something. The screams of the crowd, which had seemed endless just a moment ago, had suddenly ceased.

It was like air vanishing, like going deaf—something I'd taken for granted was suddenly gone.

I peeked out the crack beside the door, and after a second Enu joined me, standing on tiptoes to lean his chin against the top of my head.

The crowd fleeing ahead of the Enforcers had disappeared. But the thudding of the Enforcers' marching *hadn't* stopped. It had grown from a distant rumble to a constant roar, like thunderclaps so close together that the echo of one met the next striking crash.

Then the first line of Enforcers came into view out in the street: one black uniform after another, one long row after another of bubbled space helmets gleaming in the sunlight like a taunt: *You pitiful humans don't know how to fight us now. Not anymore. We've made ourselves indestructible, can't you see?*

Enu grabbed my shoulders and began to pull me away. "They'll see us!"

"No, they won't!" I shoved him away. "Only if they use the bioscans, and if those work . . ."

If those work, there's nothing we can do, nowhere we can go. No way to save ourselves.

I didn't say that out loud.

"I just want to see what they do," I whispered. "I have to know . . ."

To know if we're doomed.

Enu put his hands on my shoulders again, but only to get closer to the door. He and I both pressed our faces against the crack and kept peeking out.

One of the Enforcers at the end of the row turned toward the alley, and my heart seized. He lifted a gun to his shoulder.

I clutched Enu's hand. There wasn't time to run. I could only watch.

But the Enforcer wasn't aiming at us. He pointed his gun at the Dumpster where I'd hidden the communication device. He squeezed his trigger.

Instantly the Dumpster vanished.

"Vaporized," Enu whispered numbly. "He just va—"

"Shh," I said.

The Enforcer stepped out of line. Almost casually, he began moving toward the spot where the Dumpster had been only a moment before—and toward us. But after only five or six steps he bent down and reached for something on the ground, something alongside the broken bottles and scorched weeds.

He picked up the communication device I'd hidden there.

"Does he know we're here?" Enu asked.

"Or does he think we were in the Dumpster?" I whispered back. "Was he trying to vaporize *us*?"

Or maybe I just moved my lips and no sound came out. Maybe those words were too terrifying to say aloud.

The Enforcer pocketed the communication device and turned back toward the rest of his squad. Did he glance our way first? His shadowy bubble helmet made it impossible to see.

"Kiandra? Enu? What are you doing? Aren't you coming with us?"

It was Edwy, calling up from the bottom of the stairway. Enu and I both reached for the door handle, but my hand was a little closer. I pulled the door all the way shut, waiting to hear the lock click into place before I turned. Enu's eyes met mine as he also spun around. And even though we had only a few weeks of experience with having a younger brother—and less than twenty-four hours of knowing the other four kids—it was like Enu and I were in instant agreement: *We can't tell Edwy or the others what we saw. It will scare them too much.*

"Just double-checking the lock, pipsqueak," Enu said. His voice cracked, split with fear. He might as well have screamed, *I just saw the most horrifying thing of my life! And it wasn't a video game, wasn't a movie, wasn't special effects— it really happened.*

Edwy just nodded.

"It's like a maze down here," he said. "Kiandra, do you have any idea which way we should go?"

My feet found the first step down. My brain liked that. It was screaming, *Get away from the Enforcers and their vaporizers! Go! Go! Go!* But all I said aloud was, "We're under the biggest grocery store in Ref City. Let's aim for their storeroom. We'll need food."

"Oh, yeah. Food," Enu echoed blankly, as if he barely even knew what that was.

Enu was fifteen. I'd seen him eat two large pizzas and twenty buffalo wings, then stand up and announce, "Okay, now I'm hungry again. Did you order anything else, or are you trying to starve me?"

He *never* forgot about food.

"So do you know where the storeroom is?" Edwy asked, as if I was the one being slow and stupid.

Automatically I reached for my phone.

"Are you sure you want to do that?" Enu whispered beside me.

I did. I didn't. What I *really* wanted was to go back to yesterday, when I didn't know much of anything about Enforcers. I wanted to be back then, and back in our penthouse apartment on the other side of Ref City, where the biggest thing I'd ever had to worry about was faking Enu's grades on the school website. That and figuring out how far it was safe to push Udans, the man who was our only link to our parents, and . . .

Oh, Udans.

My heart threatened to split wide open. Maybe it *did* break apart. The last time we'd seen him, Udans was driving a truck with six unconscious Enforcers hidden in the back. He was driving it *away* from all of us kids, because he wanted us to be safe.

If the Enforcers could track down the one solitary

disarmed communication device I'd carried off, they could certainly track down Udans and the missing Enforcers.

And if they vaporized a mere Dumpster, then . . .

I stumbled on the stairs, and Enu grabbed my arm to keep me from falling.

"I don't think my phone will work this far underground—and I should probably keep the battery for urgent uses. But if I remember the building layout right, you should turn to the left," I told Edwy.

"Okay," Edwy said.

Just a matter of hours ago, Edwy had been alone and surrounded by Enforcers. And *he'd* figured out what to do, how to outsmart the Enforcers, how to get Udans to help. If a twelve-year-old could outsmart the Enforcers, couldn't the brilliant leaders of Refuge City figure out a way to convince the Enforcers to leave?

Of course they can, I told myself. *So, really, all we have to do is hang out in the Emporium of Food storeroom eating like kings for a day or two, and then everything will go back to normal. The Enforcers will leave. And Ref City will go back to being its usual glitzy, beautiful, safe, sterile place. Where nothing I do actually matters.*

I didn't usually lie to myself. But it felt like I had to now, just to keep my feet moving.

Enu and I got to the bottom of the stairs, and we followed

the younger kids through a narrow, dirty hallway lit only by bare, fly-specked bulbs. The soles of my sandals kept sticking to the dark floor, and I tried not to think about what filth might be down there. Spilled milk? Squashed bits of rotten fruit?

Blood?

Rosi and Zeba both seemed to be tiptoeing. Rosi swayed under Bobo's weight. Earlier today *she'd* been running through the desert, desperately trying to escape from the Enforcers and get Cana and Bobo to safety.

"Bobo, you're a big boy," I said. "Why don't you get down and walk on your own?"

I tried to sound kind and cajoling like Mrs. Koseet, the nicest nanny Enu and I had ever had. But somehow my voice came out harsh and angry like, well, pretty much every other nanny Enu and I had ever had.

Even in the dim light I could see Bobo tighten his grip around his sister's shoulders, bunching together the fabric of her dirty, torn dress.

"He's okay," Rosi said wearily.

I felt Cana slide her hand into mine, and I didn't shake it away.

"Somebody needs to turn on a brighter light," Bobo complained. "Or we need windows. I can't *see*."

"Kiddo, we're in a basement," Enu said. His voice was as harsh as mine. "Basements don't have windows."

Looking for another great book?
Find it
IN THE MIDDLE.

Fun, fantastic books for kids
in the in-be**TWEEN** age.

IntheMiddleBooks.com

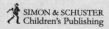